Angus's hot look pinned her feet to the floor, and she felt like a bug under a microscope.

"I want to know why you didn't contact me, given our chemistry. You said you would, and I don't think you are a woman who goes back on your word, so why didn't you call me or send me an email?"

She started to explain, but he rolled right over her. "But, mostly, I want to know why you didn't tell me about them."

He pulled a photograph from his back pocket and Thadie gasped, going hot and cold. She recognized the photo as one she'd pinned to the fridge months ago. Gus and Finn had put their plastic-molded motorbikes in their bubble bath and were sitting on them, laughing like loons. The photo had always lived on the fridge, along with takeout menus and magnets, and honestly, she'd forgotten it was there.

He'd not only noticed the photo but had managed to remove and pocket it without her or her brothers noticing. Impressive in a slightly James Bond, scary, superspy way.

Right, well, her secret was out.

Scandals of the Le Roux Wedding

Will the bride say "I do"?

Thadie Le Roux's society wedding is set to be the biggest and most lavish South Africa has ever seen! Her twin billionaire brothers, Jago and Micah, will spare no expense, because family is everything *and* they have the Le Roux name to uphold.

And that certainly helps when things start to go wrong! A scathing social media campaign here, a canceled venue there... Will Thadie ever make it down the aisle? Not least considering all the Le Rouxs are about to discover that for a union to be binding, it must first be forged in red-hot attraction!

Read Jago and Dodi's story in
The Billionaire's One-Night Baby

Discover Micah and Ella's story in
The Powerful Boss She Craves

Check out Thadie and Angus's story in
The Twin Secret She Must Reveal

All available now!

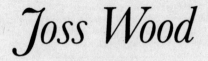

Joss Wood

THE TWIN SECRET SHE MUST REVEAL

HARLEQUIN
PRESENTS

HARLEQUIN®
PRESENTS™

Recycling programs
for this product may
not exist in your area.

ISBN-13: 978-1-335-58399-4

The Twin Secret She Must Reveal

Harlequin Enterprises ULC
22 Adelaide St. West, 41st Floor
Toronto, Ontario M5H 4E3, Canada
www.Harlequin.com

Printed in U.S.A.

Joss Wood loves books and traveling—especially to the wild places of southern Africa and, well, anywhere. She's a wife, a mom to two teenagers and a slave to two cats. After a career in local economic development, she now writes full-time. Joss is a member of Romance Writers of America and Romance Writers of South Africa.

Books by Joss Wood

Harlequin Presents

The Rules of Their Red-Hot Reunion

Scandals of the Le Roux Wedding

The Billionaire's One-Night Baby
The Powerful Boss She Craves

South Africa's Scandalous Billionaires

How to Undo the Proud Billionaire
How to Win the Wild Billionaire
How to Tempt the Off-Limits Billionaire

Harlequin Desire

Wrong Brother, Right Kiss
Lost and Found Heir
The Secret Heir Returns
Crossing Two Little Lines

Visit the Author Profile page
at Harlequin.com for more titles.

CHAPTER ONE

THIS WAS IT. In an hour she'd be married.

Thadie Le Roux glanced at her elaborate wedding dress on the double bed and touched the platinum-blonde micro braids threaded into her hair and twisted into an elegant knot at the back of her neck.

After numerous setbacks, insane press attention and her two brothers falling in love during the process, they were almost at the finish line. In a couple of hours, she'd be Mrs Clyde Strathern.

Was Clyde, ensconced in another suite down the hallway of this house, excited?

She wasn't. Not particularly. Then again, the last time she'd felt butterflies-in-her-stomach, gut-churning, light-headed excitement had been that night in London four years ago, when she'd, uncharacteristically, allowed a gorgeous stranger to join her in her hotel room and take her to bed.

He'd been a once-in-a-lifetime collision, and

their coming together gave her the best gift of her life, her twin sons, Gus and Finn. *You can't think about Angus, Thadie, not on your wedding day.*

Tightening the belt of her short dressing gown, she sat down on the edge of the huge bed, staring at her stupidly expensive wedding dress. The doubts she'd had over the past three months rolled over her and her breathing turned shallow, her skin prickling with dread. What was she doing? Clyde didn't love her, she didn't love him…

Thadie forced herself to calm down, pushing her doubts and concerns away. *You know why you are getting married, Le Roux, it was a carefully thought-out decision, remember?*

On a practical level, Clyde had agreed to pitch in with her boys, which meant more 'me' time for her. For years she'd been glued to the twins and she, maybe, wanted to return to work, and start designing again. Part-time, of course.

And yeah, providing her boys with a dad made her feel a little less guilty about wanting to do something for herself. They needed a father, and rugby superstar and national hero Clyde, both sporty and smart, was a good choice.

They moved in the same circles, had met at an event. She couldn't even remember what for now. And, unlike her tempestuous, volatile parents, Clyde was laid-back, nothing ever ruffled him. Being around him felt as if she were sailing consistently calm waters.

It was a simple transaction: Clyde liked her high profile and wanted to be part of the famous Le Roux family. She wanted a father for her boys, to shed the loneliness and responsibility of being a single mum. She knew she'd never crave his love and, provided he kept his promise to help raise Gus and Finn, he'd never disappoint her.

Could she be blamed for wanting her boys to have a stable, old-fashioned, two-parents-who-were-involved-in-their-lives upbringing? Clyde had agreed to take on that challenge.

She winced, thinking that Clyde hadn't spent much time with the twins lately, and she suddenly wondered whether helping her raise them was something he still wanted to do. No, she was overreacting. Clyde would've said something if he had any doubts about marrying her.

Admittedly, the last few months had been horrible. She'd had her first wedding venue cancelled by an unknown person, and for a while they'd been without a venue to host what was being dubbed South Africa's Wedding of the Year. She'd had journalists publicly questioning their commitment to each other, people trolling her on social media, and she'd had to ask

Clyde's stepsister, Alta, to step down as a bridesmaid due to her constant negativity. Despite a few arguments, and many tears caused by stress and frustration—hers, not Clyde's, he'd been unfazed by all the drama—they'd made it to their wedding day.

She was just stressed, being overly dramatic. It was fine, they were fine. *Everything* was *fine*.

Thadie lifted her head as her best friend, Dodi, walked into the room. As the owner of a bridal salon, Dodi had helped her choose her wedding dress. Thadie was, if she was honest, a little jealous that Dodi worked in the fashion industry when she had studied fashion design and had once had big plans to be the next Stella McCartney or Vera Wang.

Instead of making garments, she'd made babies.

'Is Liyana here?' Thadie asked her, thinking of her glamorous mother. 'She promised she would be.'

Dodi frowned and shook her head. 'She sent a message saying she'd go directly to the church.'

Despite having known Liyana would let her down, Thadie still felt disappointed, a little wounded. Her mum had never kept a promise in her life, and had never really been a mum to her in the traditional sense, so why did she expect something different on her wedding day?

It would never occur to the ex-supermodel that her wedding day was one of those iconic mother-daughter moments that was supposed to be treasured.

'Stupid of me to think that she'd put herself out,' Thadie murmured. 'Then again, if my dad was still alive, he'd probably forget he was walking me down the aisle and he'd have to be dragged off the golf course.'

Or out of one of his many mistresses' beds. Her father being a serial cheater was another disappointment. Then again, her mother hadn't been that hot on monogamy either.

Between her parents, not knowing Angus's surname and losing his unexamined business card—resulting in her not being able to contact him after their mind-blowing night together, or when she'd found out she was pregnant—she was done with being disappointed. It was far better to keep her expectations low and, above all, realistic.

'Dammit,' Dodi muttered, her attention on something happening outside the window.

Thadie stood up. 'What's going on?'

When Thadie moved to stand next to her, Dodi threw out her arm, keeping her back. 'There's a commotion at the gate. It's a fair distance away but I can see photographers, some with long-range lenses.'

No, that couldn't be right. To keep the press away, she'd arranged for a text message to be sent to their guests at the end of the church service telling them where to head for the reception.

Only a few people knew the location of the reception and she trusted most of them with her life. Thadie, still dressed in her short, silky dressing gown, crossed the room and yanked open the door to the adjacent living room. Her boys, thankfully, were with Jabu, Hadleigh House's long-term butler and the twins' honorary grandfather.

Ignoring her brothers and their fiancées and Alta, Clyde's stepsister, Thadie turned to her bodyguard—she'd opted for some personal protection due to the amount of press attention she was receiving—and asked Greg to fetch Clyde from his suite down the hallway. It was urgent.

A minute later Clyde stepped into the room but, instead of looking at her, he shoved his hands into the pockets of his tuxedo trousers and stared at the carpet. He'd clearly been expecting trouble. *Interesting.*

'We have photographers outside the gates,' Thadie stated, turning to face Clyde and Alta, ignoring her anger-induced shakes. 'I made it clear I wanted this venue to remain secret until after the church service, that I didn't want to be swarmed by the press. Yet here they are. Which one of you leaked the venue?'

The pale blonde tossed her magazine aside and rose to her feet. She picked up her flute of champagne and downed its contents. 'I did,' she admitted, without a hint of remorse.

Nobody looked surprised at that revelation. 'I figured,' Thadie said through gritted teeth. Alta had made it very clear she wasn't a fan of their union. 'Why?'

Alta exchanged a look with Clyde. He walked to the drinks trolley, poured a slug of whiskey into a crystal tumbler and tossed it back. When he turned again, his eyes connected with Alta, who nodded her encouragement.

Encouragement for what?

'I gave her permission to leak the venue,' Clyde admitted.

'Why?' Thadie whispered, shocked to her core.

Clyde looked at Alta and, being the good soldier she was, she stepped into the battle. 'Clyde and I hoped it would finally cause you to call off the wedding.'

What was happening? This was all so surreal.

Thadie saw both her brothers had stepped forward, their faces stormy, and she lifted her hand to hold them back. This was her fight, her problem to solve. 'I'm sorry to be dense, but are you saying you *don't* want to marry me, Clyde?'

Clyde pushed a frustrated hand through his hair. 'Of course I don't! We've been trying to get this wedding cancelled for weeks, but nothing we've done has succeeded in getting you to call it off!'

'Here's a novel idea—why didn't you just tell Thadie you didn't want to get married?' Micah demanded, looking furious.

Fair point.

'Why go to the hassle of having the venue cancelled, the leaks to the press about Alta being dropped as a bridesmaid, about your relationship?' Jago asked, his tone Arctic-blizzard cold.

'Clyde's brand is built on him being the good guy, the nice guy, the perfect gentleman. I didn't want his reputation tarnished,' Alta explained. 'As his publicist, that's of paramount importance. Thadie is part of the Le Roux dynasty, South African royalty,' she continued. 'She's been famous, and adored, by the public since she was tiny. You and Micah have clout and influence and are exceedingly popular as well. Clyde getting engaged to Thadie was PR gold and gave him incredible exposure. The plan was always to break up with her after six months or so.'

Right, so he'd *never* intended to marry her, to be a dad to her sons.

'I'm still not getting why you'd sabotage your wedding when a simple "I'm not interested any more" would do,' Micah stated.

'Clyde was about to break it off, but then he received an offer from a famous, family-orientated brand to be their spokesperson. It's a deal worth millions and it took months to negotiate. But he can't be associated with any scandal, he has to keep his nose clean. Breaking up with you, Thadie, the nation's princess, would've been problematic. But if *you* jilted *him*, public sympathy would be with Clyde.'

Wow. Okay, then. Thadie shook her head in disbelief.

'If you'd explained all this to me, Clyde, we could've found a solution together. But to go behind my back, to cause me, and my family, untold hours of stress is unforgivable. Micah even spent weeks out of town looking for another venue for us and Ella found this place despite all odds! Jago and Micah have paid for this wedding in advance!'

'That doesn't matter,' Micah murmured.

'It does matter!' Thadie yelled. 'And it all could've been avoided if you were honest with me, Clyde! And don't get me started on the promises you made to my boys.'

Clyde lifted one shoulder in a half-baked shrug. And the small gesture, his dismissal of her boys and their feelings, sent her revving into the red zone.

'They are spoiled brats anyway, and they don't like rugby,' Clyde said, sounding deeply bored. Who was this man? Why hadn't she seen this side of him before? Or had she ignored what she didn't like because she'd been so damn determined to snag a father for her sons?

'They are *three*!'

'Really? I thought they were older. Anyway… so Alta is ready to face the press, she'll tell them you're calling off the wedding.'

Uh…*no*.

In a couple of sentences, he'd managed to insult her as a mother—she'd worked damn hard to make sure her kids were not spoiled!—and show her he was clueless about her kids. And he still thought she'd save his precious deal?

How had she been so blind? How had she fallen for his lies to the point where she'd agreed to marry him?

It wasn't often she lost her temper or acted irrationally, but he'd pushed all her buttons. Nobody messed with her kids and their emotions. Or played her for a fool.

She was done talking. It was time for action. She spun around, and half ran out of the room, heading for the stairs. She was dimly aware of being followed and within seconds she was at the front door of the grand Victorian mansion.

'Thads, you're in a short, very revealing dressing gown,' Dodi shouted from somewhere behind her. 'And you're not wearing any shoes! Where are you going?'

She wrenched the door front door open and stepped onto the portico, facing the press who'd gathered at the gate at the end of the long driveway. From this distance, the long-range cameras would get some good photographs of her, but that wasn't enough.

She had an ex-fiancé she needed to throw under the bus.

In his Canary Wharf penthouse office on Monday afternoon, Angus Docherty kicked up his feet and rested his size thirteens on the corner of his desk, his eyes on the screen of his tablet in his lap. He'd recently returned from Pakistan, having completed an off-the-grid mission, and he had mountains of work to do.

The world didn't stop because he'd been unavailable for the past few weeks. Despite owning and operating an international, multibillion-pound company focusing on securing people, assets, and premises, he also carried out sensitive missions for western governments…missions that were dangerous, off the books and top secret.

Once a soldier, always a soldier.

It was still a source of amusement that owning and operating a business had never been on his radar growing up. No, like his father and grandfather, and great-grandfather, he'd been destined for military service, expected to match his father's and grandfather's illustrious achievements. His great-grandfather retired as a colonel, his grandfather died a few days after being promoted to major general.

Of all his army-serving ancestors, it was his father who'd attained the highest rank, the youngest general in fifty years. General Colm Docherty answered only to God. And, sometimes, to the Prime Minister. He was a legend in military circles, respected and revered. He had a tireless work ethic and was disciplined and focused. The General was a hard man to work for, he demanded his pound of flesh.

From his son, he demanded that pound of flesh, his spine, and his internal organs too.

If The General was difficult to deal with at work, he was ten times worse at home, pedantic and unemotional, relentlessly demanding. His only child was held to a higher standard than everyone else. Angus had to run faster, work harder, achieve more, and be better. Be the best.

Acceptance by his father meant he had to be perfect. Failure was not tolerated. Ever.

Catching a bullet in his thigh, which narrowly missed his femoral artery but shattered his femur, was his biggest failure of all. Being shot not only derailed his father's plans for him to be the second general bearing the Docherty name but fundamentally changed his relationship with his parents. The pins in his thigh were enough for him to be discharged from the military, a blow he still felt today. He'd had no wish to be promoted to a desk job, but leaving his unit was a wound he'd yet to recover from...

And his leaving the military was, to The General, the worst of failures. Dochertys were soldiers, and if you no longer served under the Queen's command, you were *nothing*. Up to that point, Angus had believed his parents, on some level, loved him.

He rubbed his hand over his face, thinking he was more tired than he realised if he was walking down memory lane, thinking about his estranged parents. He yawned and stretched, pushing his hands through his thick hair, overly long from spending weeks on the road.

A rap on his door had him looking up and he waved his second in command to come in. They'd served together in the unit, and Heath was the first person Angus employed when he'd established Docherty Security.

Heath, his tablet in his hand, dropped into the visitor's chair. Angus caught the smile on Heath's normally taciturn face and wondered what was making his dour friend smile. 'What's up?' he asked.

Heath shook his head, his mouth twitching in amusement. 'I'm watching a video of a South African client. She got dumped shortly before her wedding and her impromptu press conference has gone viral.'

Angus dropped his legs and took the tablet, tapping his finger against the play button. The woman wore a silky dressing gown, edged by six inches of white lace at the cuffs at the wrists and hem, revealing most of her thighs and long, gorgeous legs. The top of her dressing gown gaped open and he, and the rest of the world, caught a glimpse of a luscious breast, covered by a strapless, lacy, pale blue bra.

He moved on to her face, and he stilled, every nerve in his body frozen. Thadie…

Angus felt his heart rate increasing—something that rarely happened—and he drummed his fingers on his thigh. He never lost his cool but one look at her lovely face and tall, sexy, curvy body had his core temperature increasing.

He'd been in firefights, had bombs explode

around him, fought for his life in hand-to-hand combat, been *shot* and he never lost his cool. One look into her extraordinary eyes and he was a basket case.

Angus lifted his finger to trace her cut-glass cheekbones, her pointy chin and lush mouth. Her eyes were almond-shaped and as dark as sin, and her skin reminded him of a topaz pendant his grandmother wore, rich and a golden brown. There were freckles on her nose and dotting her cheeks and he recalled trying to kiss every one he found on her body. Not, in any way, a hardship. In the video she wore thin, long, bright blonde braids—they suited her—but he remembered her having springy coils touching her shoulders.

Angus pushed play and her rich voice rolled over him.

'I came here to tell you my fiancé, ex-fiancé,' she corrected, holding up a finger, 'has not only dumped me but has just admitted to sabotaging the plans we made for our wedding. He did that in the hope the stress of multiple wedding disasters would cause me to call it off because he didn't have the guts to do it himself.'

Her chest rose up and fury caused her cheeks to glow with a pink undertone. She was hopping mad and, man, she was stunning. Then Thadie placed the balls of her hands into her eye sockets and pushed down. After a few seconds, she lowered her hands, but he caught no sign of tears.

'He told me he intended to blame me in the court of public opinion for the break-up so I'm out here, telling you I'd planned on getting married today, that I was *prepared* to become his wife.'

Prepared? That was an unusual turn of phrase and one that didn't imply she was wildly in love with the groom. Angus watched, fascinated, as two tall men approached her—alike enough for him to think they were twins—dressed in designer suits and, judging by the roses in their lapels, part of the wedding party. They also exuded a proprietary and protective air.

One of the men draped his jacket around her shoulders, hiding her body from the cameras. Then he wrapped his arm around her and led her back to the house. The other stood in front of the press corps, who were lapping up the drama.

'As most of you know, I'm Jago Le Roux. As stated, my sister's wedding has been cancelled,' he said, his expression grim. 'I'd ask you to respect our privacy and give her space to work through this day and drama, but I suspect that's not going to happen, is it?'

A barrage of questions punctured the air as he followed his siblings back to the house. The video cut off and Angus, still shaken but trying to hide it, lifted his eyes to look at Heath.

'Explain,' he demanded.

Heath stretched out his long legs and rested his hands on his stomach. 'We were hired to protect one of Johannesburg's most recognisable faces, the heiress Thadie Le Roux—'

Her first name, he recalled her telling him, meant 'loved one' in Zulu. It was an unusual name and one he'd never heard before or since that night in London four years ago. Memories of gliding his hands over her silky, glorious skin, exploring her sexy mouth, her gasps and her groans as he loved her, bombarded him. Those six hours spent with her were the best sexual memories of his life, and it took all his willpower to keep his expression impassive.

'This is a massive story in South Africa and, as a result, Docherty Security is attracting attention down there. It's been forty-eight hours since the wedding was called off, but the ex-fiancé is, in the hope of rehabilitating his reputation, doing interviews. His actions are fuelling the story and keeping it in the headlines. Now the international press corps has picked up the story and, because her mother is a famous ex-supermodel and socialite, the attention on her is going to double. Or triple.'

Angus listened to him, only one part of

his brain focused on what he was saying. He couldn't believe he'd found her, that he knew now who she was, her surname, where she lived. Four years ago, on meeting each other at an engagement party, they'd left the party separately and met up on the pavement below the couple's penthouse apartment. He'd invited her out for a drink but somehow, in the taxi from the party to the bar, they'd started kissing and she'd instructed the taxi driver to take them to her hotel suite.

All their conversation from that point on had been done with hands and lips, with strokes and kisses. They'd agreed, only first names, nothing more. Their attraction and chemistry had been mind-blowing, overlaid with an intensity he'd never experienced before. For the first time, instead of running out of the door after a sexual encounter, he had been desperate for more time with her. In a day or two, he'd reasoned, definitely by the time she was due to leave London in four days, he'd be ready to say goodbye. Because he always, always said goodbye. Back then—and now—he had sky-high emotional barriers and a gorgeous foreigner wasn't going to punch through them.

As always, he hadn't had the time, or the inclination, to make space for a woman in his life and seventy-two hours had seemed enough time to get her out of his system.

Over breakfast the next morning, he'd invited her to stay with him for the rest of her time in London, and, to his surprise, she'd accepted. Because she'd lost her phone the night before, they'd agreed she'd check out of the hotel, find a store and replace her phone. And he'd take her suitcase with him to his office. When she was done, she'd call him—he'd placed his business card on the bedside table—and he'd give her directions to his flat, and he'd meet her there, and they'd spend the rest of the day in bed.

The phone call never came and her suitcase still sat at the back of his walk-in closet. In the days following their encounter, he'd tried to find her, but soon realised it was an impossible endeavour when he only knew her first name.

But he knew more now.

It was a ten, twelve-hour flight to Johannesburg and if he flew out later, after his dinner meeting with an important client, he could be there by mid-afternoon, South African time, tomorrow.

No! Flying to South Africa was a ridiculous notion. She was a one-night stand, nothing more.

'Her family has an incredibly high profile, and she has a huge social media following. Her brothers recommended us to their younger sister when she expressed a need for a personal protection officer. I'm worried that if something happens to her, if she so much as kicks her toe, Docherty Security is going to catch flak. I think she needs more PPOs. She might not agree to pay for more bodyguards, might not want them, but this is a nightmare waiting to happen.'

Angus nodded his agreement. He understood Heath's worry about reputational damage, it was normally at the forefront of his mind too. But not today.

Yes, he'd been crazy attracted to her, and the memories of that night were seared onto his brain. But attraction wasn't driving his need to see her—his curiosity was. After four years of wondering, he might finally get answers to questions that still, occasionally, kept him awake at night. What had happened after she'd climbed into the taxi outside her hotel? Why had she changed her mind? Had she had second thoughts? If she'd decided not to see him again, why hadn't she contacted him to collect her suitcase?

How had she gone from passionately kissing him on the pavement to vanishing?

He wasn't interested in rebooting their affair, in picking up where they'd left off. He just wanted to know, *dammit*. He'd always been able to read people and situations and this ability had saved his life on more than one occasion. Where had he gone so wrong with Thadie?

He'd always been the type to dig, to understand, to gather every bit of knowledge about a situation so he had a clear, objective view of the events. She was an unsolved puzzle, an incomplete mission, an end that hadn't been securely tied. As a soldier, and a perfectionist, Angus hated unresolved questions.

He'd read her wrong and her not contacting him felt like a failure. And failure, as his father had drummed into him from the day he could understand the concept, was unacceptable.

But was he really going to fly thousands of miles and incur the running costs of his intercontinental jet just to ascertain how, and why, he'd read her wrong? Yes, he wanted to know how. And why. It wasn't wounded pride, or ego: the reality was that if he misconstrued another situation during an undercover operation or misinterpreted another person in a dangerous situation, people, including himself, could get hurt or killed. The worst failure of all.

There was also a good chance that when he got to South Africa, once he laid eyes on her, he'd wonder why he'd built her up in his mind, why he'd spent so much mental energy on one long-ago night. There was no chance she would carry the same punch she had years ago.

But he'd have the answers to his questions, and, since he was rich, he could easily afford the costs he'd incur. While he was there he'd also address the issue of Docherty Security suffering reputational damage, by arranging and swallowing the costs of additional protection officers for Thadie.

In a couple of days, he'd never have to give her another thought.

It was a plan with a solid outcome, one that had no chance of failing.

Angus liked plans. And he never failed.

CHAPTER TWO

THADIE COULDN'T BELIEVE that she had walked out of Cathcart House in her skimpy dressing gown, showing a lot of leg and, because she hadn't thought to tighten the sash, the edges of her baby-blue strapless bra. Standing up in front of all those reporters and setting out, in excruciating detail, Clyde's perfidy had been a stupid move and she was now paying the price. For the past three days, she'd had reporters standing outside her gate and dogging her every move.

As the only daughter of one of the country's richest men and a famous ex-supermodel, she was a society column regular and her engagement to a World Cup rugby superstar and national hero had been wildly reported on. Her wedding planning woes and the speculation about the health of her and Clyde's relationship had kept her in the media spotlight. She and Clyde had been keeping South Africans entertained for months.

Thadie had spent almost every moment since leaving Cathcart House examining the last nine months, trying to understand how she'd ended up unengaged in such a dramatic fashion. She'd genuinely thought Clyde would be a good father for Gus and Finn and, in their early days together, he had spent time with them, playing with them and getting to know them. Had she clung onto those memories as proof he'd be a good father and, caught up in the drama of their wedding going wrong, ignored or excused his lack of attention towards the twins? She bit her lip. Maybe.

Probably.

She'd spent her childhood and teens wishing, longing and hoping for her parents' attention so when Clyde had said he'd be the twins' dad, her eyes had filled with stars. She'd been so enamoured with giving the twins the stable family she'd never had that she'd ignored and dismissed anything that didn't fit into her fantasy of a perfect family.

She'd been so focused on netting them a father that she hadn't paid enough attention to the quality, and the qualities, of her catch. Too much fantasy, not enough reality.

Thadie sighed, feeling exhausted, wishing she were less obsessed with her need to give them a father, a role model. It was, she admitted, her issue, not theirs. But the compulsion to find them a father remained.

The memory of a rough-hewn face, attractively rugged, flashed on the big screen in her mind. The twins had his eyes, a light blue-green, a compelling contrast to their pale brown skin. Gus had his long nose, Finn Angus's mouth. Being already tall for their age, they'd also, she suspected, inherited his height. Having the boys in her life was a constant reminder of the best night of her life…

If only she hadn't lost his business card. Or had even looked at it before she lost it.

And not only because she'd wanted him to know about the twins. No, from the moment their eyes had met, she'd felt connected to him. She recalled the way raindrops glistened on his rich brown hair, the way his mouth hitched in a half-smile, and his extraordinarily wide shoulders. She recalled her heart settling and sighing. Until that moment she hadn't realised she'd been waiting for him to make an appearance in her life…

No, she was not going to add to her misery by thinking of Angus, what could've been, what had been lost. If she went down that path, she'd find herself mired in misery and she was feeling downhearted enough, thank you very much.

Instead of wallowing, she needed to do something, *anything*…

The boys were with Jabu, the semi-retired butler who'd all but raised her, and she had to get out of the house. The walls were starting to close in on her. Her bodyguard Greg had tried to stop her, but Thadie overrode him, telling him that he could either accompany her or not, but she was leaving.

Greg, because it was his job, had no choice but to accompany her.

He insisted on driving, and it took him some time to manoeuvre her SUV through the throng of press at her gate. Ten minutes later, they were on the highway, heading for her best friend's bridal salon. Dodi would steer her to her office, sit her down and give her tea. Dodi wouldn't feel offended if she remained silent, or she would listen if Thadie wanted to recount every detail of the last few days. Or months. She was a truly excellent friend.

Knowing Greg would struggle to find parking near Dodi's popular salon, she told him to park a street over, not minding the walk past the art galleries, boutiques and delicatessens. She loved this area of her city. Melrose was an arty, lovely part of Johannesburg and it never bored her.

Leaving the car, she pulled her large bag over her shoulder and started walking in the direction of Love & Enchantment, Dodi's salon. Getting out of the house had been an excellent idea, she thought, as Greg fell into position behind her. She needed the exercise and maybe, if she was really lucky, she'd find a box of artisanal pastries or hand-crafted chocolates in Dodi's salon. There normally was. Dodi often calmed down overanxious, entitled or neurotic brides with sugary treats. And champagne.

She could do with a glass, or three, of champagne.

Thadie heard the beep of a text message and pulled her bag across her body, opening the zip. She pulled out her phone and pushed the sunglasses onto her head to read the message. Another publication was asking for a comment on her crazy press conference. *Was she overcome with grief? Was that why she went outside in her dressing gown?*

No, she silently replied, she had just been comprehensively, brain-shutting-down angry. Of course she'd never intended to do a press conference barefoot, dressed in an ultra-short satin-and-lace dressing gown. And if they thought she was stupid enough to give them any additional coverage by commenting on her enormous faux pas, they were the ones losing their minds.

'Thadie, I think we should go back to the car,'

Greg said, from his position behind her. 'Being out in public is a bad idea.'

Thadie looked around, thinking they were just round the corner from Dodi's salon. Maybe twenty yards, thirty? 'Let's just see,' Thadie implored him. 'I'm going berserk at home, Greg, and I need to see my best friend. It will be fine,' she assured him with more confidence than she felt. 'Dodi's place is just around the corner.'

'Why do I think I am going to regret this?' Greg muttered, moving closer to her as they turned right…

And crashed straight into a mob of flashing cameras, shouted questions and smelly, less-than-fresh reporters. They must've been waiting quietly for them, having sussed they were close by. It was an ambush, Thadie realised. The press had informants everywhere and it was possible someone had followed her car and, after deducing where she was going—she and Dodi were friends long before Dodi's engagement to her brother Jago—tipped off the press.

Greg tried to keep some distance between her and the reporters, but it wasn't possible as they circled her from all sides. The questions amalgamated into an indecipherable cacophony and, being so close, the light flashes from the cameras hurt her eyes. Thadie felt as if she were in a fairground hall of mirrors where she couldn't focus on anyone's face and had no conception of distance. She started to hyperventilate and her grip on Greg's arm tightened. At least, she hoped it was Greg's arm, she couldn't be sure.

Just when she thought she couldn't take any more, a thickly muscled forearm encircled her waist, spun her around and plastered her against a very wide and very hard chest. The arm tightened and her feet lost contact with the ground. Using his other hand, and with a series of blunt and rude commands issued in a deep, don't-test-me voice, her rescuer cleared a path out of the melee.

Thadie's body stiffened. She recognised that voice, that Scottish accent…the rolled r's, stronger vowels and softer t's. No, it couldn't be, it wasn't possible. There was no way Angus was carrying her out of this mob. It had to be another six-foot-four, ripped guy who smelled like a walk through a wild forest.

Thadie placed her hand on that hard chest and looked up. A cold wave doused her, then a blowtorch seared her skin, and she couldn't decide whether she was blisteringly hot or freezing cold. Her mouth dried up and her heart rate rocketed up and, yes, she'd suddenly acquired a hundred thousand butterflies in her stomach. And they were taking flight.

She'd experienced a couple of tough days, and

her eyes had to be playing tricks on her, because there was no way that Angus, her one-night—and exceedingly hot—stand was carrying her over to a massive, matte black Range Rover and tossing her inside.

What? How? Was she losing her mind?

But since he was the only person who'd ever made her feel light-headed, consumed by the urge to touch and taste, she might not be going crazy. Or not just yet.

From the passenger seat of his car, Thadie watched, flabbergasted, as Angus walked around the bonnet of the luxury vehicle, his scowl enough of a deterrent to make the reporters keep their distance. She was vaguely aware of Greg saying he'd drive her car home, but she couldn't tear her eyes off Angus—so masculine, so sexy!—sliding behind the wheel of the car.

Without a word, he started the car and slapped it into gear, his eyes on his side mirror, checking to see if he could pull into the traffic. 'What on earth are *you* doing here?' she asked, her voice cracking.

Those eyes, the mini version of which she looked into every day, collided with hers. The startling blue-green colour was infused with annoyance and a great deal of frustration.

'I'm protecting you, Thadie,' he said, transferring his gaze to the rear-view mirror. He waited for Greg to pass him and Thadie noticed his scowl. His displeasure with Greg oozed from every pore and Thadie felt the need to protect her young, albeit inexperienced bodyguard.

'It's not Greg's fault. I insisted on going to Dodi's place,' she gabbled. 'I told him that I'd go alone if he didn't accompany me.'

Angus's eyes returned to her, and she felt pinned to her seat as he silently debated whether she was telling the truth or not. While she waited, she noticed the strands of grey hair above his ears, and he now wore thick stubble instead of a beard. There were new lines next to his eyes. He looked older, warier, a hundred times sexier.

Thadie grabbed the skirt of her dress and twisted it in her clenched fists, feeling her heart pushing its way through her ribcage. She felt light-headed. Her thoughts were racing at two hundred miles a minute. How and why was the father of her sons sitting next to her, looking remote and distant and, man, even more handsome than he did four years ago?

Thadie looked out of the window and bit the inside of her lip, not knowing what to do. Or say. She'd just been dumped by her fiancé and was facing an insane amount of press attention.

And now she had to deal with the arrival of her one-night lover and the father of her toddlers.

She didn't know which way was up.

'I'm sorry, I don't understand why you are here,' Thadie said, sounding utterly confused.

He didn't blame her. The last person she'd expected to see was the man she'd slept with, and forgotten about, four years later in her home city, while she was being jostled by a pack of reporters looking for a headline.

Despite seeing Hadley's car ahead of him—he and that young man would be having words later about how to say no to clients—he checked his phone's directions, pulled left and was nearly cut off by a small bus, the passenger hanging out of the window, calling to pedestrians.

'I'm driving in a strange city, and I need to concentrate,' Angus told her, his voice hard. 'Can the explanations wait?'

'I suppose they'll have to,' Thadie muttered, slumping in her seat. Angus dropped his sunglasses onto his eyes, joined another stream of traffic and rubbed the back of his neck. What he most wanted to do was find a hotel, strip her out of that sexy dress and kiss his way up and down her body before sliding inside and losing himself in her.

God, it was hot in here, he needed air. But

the air conditioner was on, it was working fine. No, he was the one overheating and all because he'd, too briefly, held Thadie in his arms. Angus shoved his hand into his hair, holding back his groan of frustration. He'd thought he wanted answers, and he did, but he'd never expected this insane amount of lust, to feel so intensely, crazy attracted to her again. He was older, hopefully wiser, and he'd thought he'd outgrown his desire for her...

But...no. Not at all. If anything, it was wilder, more out of control.

Brilliant. His South African trip wasn't going to plan, and Angus felt weirdly off balance. Nothing was as he'd expected, and he felt as if he were floundering in quicksand, being battered by enormous waves. He was way out of his comfort zone, and he didn't like it.

If he'd known how seeing her again was going to affect him, he would've stayed in London. Angus didn't like feeling mentally, and emotionally shaken, or caught off guard. He'd grown up in a house where emotions were carefully regulated, if not dismissed. To achieve what he did, his father, The General, gave everything he had to the army; it was his wife and mistress, the great love affair of his life. To create his own legacy, to build an international, and respected, company, Angus needed to be as emotionally divorced as his father had been. Was.

But, unlike his father, he'd walk his road alone, he wouldn't view his wife and kids as shiny accessories, further proof he was a success in every aspect of his life. He'd watched his parents' dysfunctional marriage, had seen his friends marry and divorce, the unhappiness relationships engendered when they fell apart. What was the point of starting something that had a snowball's chance in hell of succeeding? Not succeeding at anything was unacceptable and taking on wild-goose challenges like relationships was, simply, stupidity.

He didn't believe in love. Neither did he need it, whatever *it* was…

Besides, he didn't have the space in his life for a relationship. All his energy had to be devoted to creating a legacy of his own, to prove to himself that The General wasn't the only Docherty who could achieve extraordinary things. He had a point to prove, and nothing—not even a gorgeous woman who made his heart race— would stand in his way.

Forty minutes later, Angus closed his car door, ignored the shouts and demands from the press and followed Thadie up the stone path to her front door. She plugged in a code on the panel and the door opened on hinges placed in the middle of the door. He stepped directly into a double-volume, open-plan great room. The wall to his right was covered in hats, placed to form a sweep of colour from espresso to white. The far wall comprised double-volume glass, and, on closer inspection, he realised that the wall was a sliding door opening onto an entertainment deck and sparkling pool. Indoor plants, including a vine climbing up and across a wall, supported by hooks, added pops of colour to the room. Comfortable-looking couches squatted on expensive rugs but there were no personal items or photographs on any of the surfaces. There were also blank spaces on the wall where paintings, or artwork, had hung before.

Despite it being denuded of any personal items—was it because she had intended to redecorate with her new husband?—he liked her house. It was very different from his white and black and minimalistic flat in Knightsbridge. It was, he decided, homely, unlike the perfectly neat, emotionally cold houses he'd grown up in.

His home, like everything else in his life, had been regimented. Everything had its place, and God help you if you spilt anything or used something and didn't put it back in its proper place. He didn't know if both his parents were naturally neat freaks or if his father had trained his mother to be that way, but it had been an uncomfortable way to live. Somehow, he knew Thadie wouldn't sweat the small stuff. She was the type who encouraged people to put their feet up onto her furniture, relax, and enjoy her very pretty home.

Enjoy her. After all, they were alone in her house…

Thadie placed her hands on the island counter separating the kitchen and dining area—a wooden table with bench seats sat between the kitchen and the living area—and dropped her head between her arms. Her bright braids hung down her back, pulled together by a plain black band. Her eyes were scrunched closed and he thought she was silently cursing. They were alone and they were adults—he wasn't sure why she felt the need to keep those words silent. He'd served and worked in an industry dominated by men and could cope with a swear word or two. He had more than a few creative curses of his own.

'What are you doing here, Angus?' she asked without looking up at him.

He was a straightforward guy, someone who never pulled his punches, but he didn't want to toss questions at her head or hear her explanations. Because if he got what he came here for—her explanation on how he'd read her wrong—he'd have no reason to stick around, to spend any more time in her company.

He wanted to hold her face between his hands,

lower his mouth to hers, feel her tall body aligned with his, have his thigh between her legs and his hand on her lower back, pushing her stomach into his erection.

Angus swallowed, feeling disconcerted. His attraction had come roaring back, as ferocious as a category five hurricane, as relentless as a mega-tsunami. He was, he reluctantly admitted, in big trouble here. A huge part of him didn't care about what had happened in London, he simply wanted to take up where they'd left off.

Her in his arms, both of them on their way to getting naked.

'Angus?' Right, she'd asked him a question.

'I saw the video of your impromptu press conference,' he answered her. As long as he lived, he'd never forget Thadie, dressed in that very sexy dressing gown, taking down her waste-of-space groom and exposing his conniving, behind-the-scenes shenanigans. Good for her that she hadn't curled up in a corner and wept but instead she'd come out swinging. And looked stunning doing it.

But he was here for a reason. He'd address her need for additional protection soon—he'd been met at OR Tambo International Airport by his Johannesburg manager and briefed on the drive to Rosebank, where his offices were based. Her non-wedding and her ex's idiotic denials of her statements at the press conference were feeding the tabloid newspapers and leading to a rise in people trolling her online. There had been a couple of threats levelled against her as well.

But before they discussed business, he wanted answers to why their plans had gone so badly awry. If he could work out how he'd read the situation wrong, he could avoid repeating his mistake.

'Why didn't you contact me after London? You had my business card with every number I had written on it, all my email addresses, and my company website. What happened?'

If Thadie was thrown by the new direction of their conversation she didn't show it. She tossed her head and lifted her chin, her eyes blazing. 'Why are you so certain I wanted to contact you again? It was a one-night stand, nothing special, and I decided to move on.'

Her eyes slid to the left and Angus knew she was lying. He saw the pulse beating in her long, elegant neck, and noticed the pink flush on her skin. She was trying to be insouciant, but her body gave her away; her now hard nipples pushed against the fabric of her dress's bodice, and he knew, simply knew, that under her skirt, her thighs were parted.

She wanted him, he wanted her, and their chemistry was undeniable and extraordinary. And it wasn't something that should be left unexplored. They'd been the human equivalent of

Wolf-Rayet stars, supernovas that slammed together, burned brightly and died quickly...

But, thanks to Thadie's vanishing, Angus felt as if they'd only brushed by each other instead of properly colliding. From the moment he saw her again, even before he'd hoisted her into his arms and carried her away, he'd known he was fighting a losing battle, that they'd revisit their insane attraction. It was too powerful, inevitable. It was going to happen, apparently sooner rather than later.

His questions could wait.

He crossed the room, moving quickly to stand in front of her, looking down into her lovely face, and waited for her to push him back, or to move out of his personal space. He gave her a minute, maybe more, to put some distance between them but she stayed where she was, her eyes not leaving his.

She broke first, moving closer to him, and when her breasts brushed his chest he lifted his hands to hold her upper arms, pressing his body into hers, his chest against her breasts, his thigh between her legs. She nodded, tipped her face up in a silent plea and, giving into temptation, he lowered his mouth to cover hers, desperate to revisit the intense connection they'd shared so long ago.

He'd expected a trickle of lust, maybe a small punch of want, but nothing prepared him for the thwack of passion, the hard-hitting strike of sensation. Her lips were soft, her skin under his hands silky and her mouth was pure heaven. Kissing her was the sexual equivalent of stepping into a space both comforting and intensely exciting. She tasted of mint and coffee, smelled of apple orchards and berries, of wildness itself. Thadie whimpered and he deepened the kiss, noticing, from a place far away, that her arms were around his neck, her fingers playing with his hair. His hand was, of its own volition, holding her face, his other hand gripped her butt.

He needed more, he needed *everything*. Reality was so much better than his imagination, so he pulled up the material of her dress and stroked the back of her slim thigh, up and over the bare skin of her butt cheek, barely covered by her skimpy underwear. He slid his fingers under the edge of her high-cut panties and palmed her, pulling her closer to him so that the evidence of how much he wanted her pushed deeper into her stomach.

How could she have walked away from more of this, left him before their intense attraction burned out? He needed to know why but, more than that, he needed to kiss her. Here in her kitchen, for as long as she allowed him to. She was a wild wind sweeping across a moonlit desert, beautiful and inconvenient, a blue-green sea teeming with wild underwater currents, a long drink of icy water after a twelve-mile hike across rocky terrain. She was... *God*...a woman a man crossed continents for.

And he wanted more, he wanted whatever she could give him. He deepened the kiss, needing to see her naked, to have her luscious body pressed up against his without the barrier of their clothing. He wanted unrestricted access to every inch of creamy skin, wanted his mouth on the back of her knee, her ankle, her hipbone, that special, lovely place between her thighs. And, judging by her breathy moans, the way she'd pulled his shirt out from his trousers, streaking her hands across his bare back, she wanted him the same way.

Her passion matched his and he thought it one of the best gifts he'd ever received.

'Love the way you kiss,' she muttered, tracing his lips with her tongue. 'The way you taste...'

He was about to reply, to cover her breast with his hand when he heard the front door open. He dropped Thadie to his feet and instinctively pushed her behind him, ready to face the threat.

Across the room, two tall guys entered the room and were advancing on them, their expressions stormy. A series of impressions bombarded him: fit, muscled and, maybe, a little trained. If this encounter ended up in a fight, he'd win but he'd take a hammering. But he'd, with the last breath he took, protect Thadie.

'What is going on here?' the blond man roared. 'Who are you and how do you know my sister?'

The haze created by passion was clearing, and it was all coming back to him now. He'd seen them in the video Heath had showed him. These men were Thadie's brothers. Or, more accurately, half-brothers. Same father, different mother. Owners, according to the research he'd had his assistant do, of a multibillion-dollar holding company with interests in many sectors. Rich, very rich, indeed. Along with their sister, they were South African royalty.

Thadie briefly squeezed his arm as she walked past him to the closest couch. She sat down and leaned back against its thick cushions, looking exhausted. 'Angus, meet Jago and Micah Le Roux, my brothers.'

Angus nodded at them, his mouth as dry as dust. An awkward silence descended and, spotting a glass sitting upside next to the preparation sink, he grabbed it and poured himself some water. He needed a minute, or ten.

He felt like a spinning top at the end of its revolution, about to slump sideways. He wasn't a guy who overreacted—or reacted at all—when life threw him a curveball. He'd faced bullets and bombs, terrorists and predators, relying on his training to get him out of some pretty hairy situations.

Thadie pushed him way out of his comfort zone, and he didn't know how to navigate this unfamiliar, challenging scenario. He was winging it, and for someone who loved control and feared failure, it was terrifying.

Angus, his back to Thadie and her brothers, lifted the glass to his lips, his eyes falling on the covered-with-magnets fridge. Some of the magnets were from travel destinations—New York, London, Mexico, Cape Town and numerous other cities—and some held inspirational sayings. The biggest magnet, a bright, bold cartoon pineapple, kept some takeaway menus affixed to the fridge. Angus noticed the corner of a photograph peeking out from underneath a sushi menu and, keeping his back to the others, he lifted his finger and pushed aside the menus to see two young faces staring at him.

His heart slammed into his ribcage, stuttered and spluttered. Their hair was curlier, their skin darker, but other than that the two boys—the same age but non-identical—looked, in different ways, like he did when he was a kid. And, big clue, they both had his strangely coloured eyes, that hard to find blue-green with a deeper green ring encircling the lighter colour.

They couldn't be… Surely. But were they? How? Really?

Was this actually happening?

CHAPTER THREE

THIS HAD TO be a bad dream, nothing else made sense. Any moment now she'd wake up in her lovely bed, she'd yawn and stretch and long for coffee. The boys would rush in, pile on top of her and start chattering.

Three, two, one...

But...no, her life was a trainwreck. Her brothers had almost walked in on her and Angus kissing. Would've seen Angus's hand under her dress. Kissing? That was such a small word for what they'd done; they'd consumed each other. And yes, he was right, dammit, their chemistry was off the charts. Hot, crazy, inexplicable.

And, worst of all, she *still* didn't know why he was in South Africa. Their one night together wasn't reason enough for him to cross continents, she wasn't a femme fatale who lured men across oceans. And he couldn't possibly know about the twins...

The twins! Thadie resisted the urge to put her

face in her hands. Angus was their *father*. And
he was here.

In the months and years after the birth, she'd
often cursed the fact that she'd lost his business card, the only means she had to contact
him. She'd tried to find him but had had no idea
where to start. All she had was his first name.
She often wished she could tell him that he'd
helped make the extraordinary creatures who
were her sons.

What would have happened if she had? On
hearing that she was pregnant, would he have
offered to marry her? Even if he hadn't, she
couldn't see him running, leaving her to cope
on her own. She could've given up her internship
in New York, stayed in London, maybe at his
place, maybe at her own. He would've attended
antenatal classes with her, been with her when
she went for check-ups, and been in the deliv-
ery room when she tried, and failed, to push out
his sons. His would've been the first face she
saw when she came around after her C-section,
him holding both babies, introducing her to his
sons. He would've helped with nappy changes
and midnight feeds, rocking to sleep.

Would he have been there for her…? And,
more importantly, been there for Gus and Finn.

Unlike her parents, who'd had as little to do
with her as they possibly could. She recalled so

many occasions when she'd demanded their attention, and their promises to stay home more, or take her to the movies, to the beach, or simply to spend quality, family time with her. She couldn't remember one promise they'd kept, any time they'd spent with her, or them taking her on a family, kid-centric holiday.

As a result, she'd dreamed of what she'd never witnessed, a couple raising their kids, shared responsibilities, double the joy. She'd imagined a strong shoulder to rest her head on, someone to listen and to love her, to make her the centre of his world. Being the focus of someone's love and attention…

But after the twins had come along, she hadn't had the time and energy to dream any more. Her entire life was focused on her boys. She'd done everything herself, feeding and changing nappies, rocking two howling babies to sleep, one in each arm, constantly tired, increasingly overwhelmed. She'd come through it and her rose-coloured glasses had been ripped off.

She was a mum and her wants and needs weren't important, her sons came first.

And now their father, their *real* father, was back on the scene and she had no idea how Angus would respond to that bombshell. More importantly, would Angus even want to play an active part in their lives and, if he did, would he be a good father to Gus and Finn?

Hold your horses, Le Roux. You are still assuming that Angus would've wanted to play a part in the twins' lives, assuming he would've stepped up to the plate. But you don't, actually, know.

She'd made so many mistakes with Clyde, she might have made wrong assumptions about Angus too. What she wanted to believe wasn't necessarily the truth.

Angus did have the right to know about the twins, but his rights would always take second place to what was best for her sons. He'd dropped back into her life not even an hour before. She needed some time to think, gather her emotions and, most importantly, find a way to stop herself from throwing her very willing body against his.

Jago's irate voice penetrated her hurly-burly thoughts. 'Will someone tell us what on earth is going on?'

When her eyes met Angus's, his were unreadable. 'I'm not quite sure what Angus is doing here, to be honest,' Thadie told them truthfully. 'We met years ago, and earlier he rescued me from a press mob outside Dodi's salon.'

'The press knew she was going to be there. She's being followed. Or tracked,' Angus said.

'The personal protection officer who works for me—what you call a bodyguard—should never have taken her there. It was a stupid move.'

His eyes held no warmth and Thadie felt as if he'd caught her shoplifting or joyriding. He had an air of authority that had her bossy brothers eying him with caution. Her brothers were international businessmen, and few people managed to put that hint of wariness in their eyes.

Micah's eyebrows rose. '*Your* PPO officer?'

'My name is Angus Docherty, and I own Docherty Security. Thadie is a client through my Johannesburg branch.'

Thadie watched as Angus crossed the room and held out his hand. Micah shook his hand, and then Jago did the same.

'You own the security company?' she demanded. His surname meant nothing to her. She'd never known it. When she'd been looking for a bodyguard, she'd taken her brothers' recommendation to hire someone from Docherty Security, reputed to be one of the best companies in the world, without looking into it too closely. She'd been desperate and she trusted her brothers.

In the world...

Which meant he owned and operated a huge, multinational company.

If she'd paid attention to anything other than

his spectacular body and sexy face, she would've noticed the fancy watch on his wrist, his designer shoes and his expensive haircut. But no, all her focus had been on when next she could taste him. No one, before or since, made her feel so out of control.

She wasn't, she admitted, a fan of the wild emotions he whipped up. When her parents had been around, they'd fought often and with wild abandon. Volatile was too tame a word for their top-of-their-lungs fights. As a result, she did not enjoy feeling anything less than calm and in control. Especially now that she had kids. How could functional relationships be tempestuous, irrational, and loud? That was why she had felt safe with Clyde—he was the least volatile person she knew. Even when he'd been breaking things off with her, he'd been completely calm.

Sneaky and deceitful? Sure. Stormy? Never.

How could relationships be a wild wind and a tempestuous sea and still be considered healthy? No, she had danced on the banks of those rough winds, and she knew what she was talking about. Thanks to her parents, she believed love and passion involved shouting and objects being thrown. Ugly words had been followed by her parents slinking upstairs, hostility having turned to passion. Yelling and shouting had turned them on, but neither of them had given a thought to the little girl sitting at the bottom of the stairs, crying and confused. She would not do that to the twins, to herself. She would not raise them in a house where they felt bewildered and scared, unable to identify what love, like, and respect looked and sounded like. Clyde was a coward, but he was never sarcastic or ugly and he never raised his voice. She'd spent so little time with Angus and she had no idea of the person he really was. Until she figured that out, she'd keep the twins a secret from him.

Thadie remained seated as Micah made coffee—he was as at home in her kitchen as she was in the one at Hadleigh House, her childhood home they were currently renovating into two separate houses—which Angus refused. Her brothers sat down opposite her, but Angus remained standing, preferring to loom over them, his big arms crossed and biceps straining the bands of his shirt.

Thadie tried to ignore him, but it was impossible. He was too big, too unapproachable, far too sexy. Taking a deep breath, she lifted her coffee cup to her lips and took what she hoped was a reviving sip. She saw a million questions in her brothers' eyes and hoped they weren't going to ask her any—she couldn't cope with getting a third-degree interrogation.

But she did want to know why they were in

her house on a Tuesday afternoon. They were exceptionally busy men.

'The press attention around you is ridiculous,' Jago said, placing his ankle on his opposite knee. 'Not only are they calling us at all hours, but they are also camping outside Hadleigh House and at work.'

Thadie placed her palm on her forehead. Her impulsive press conference was the gift that kept on giving. Nobody else should've been affected but her. Not her kids, not her brothers and not her best friends. But she had no idea how to get the reporters to back off. Another press conference would just keep their attention on her and asking for privacy was like asking for a platinum-plated moon. All she could do was apologise, which she did again.

Jago shook his head. 'We need a solution.'

Angus brushed past her legs to sit down next to her on the couch. Although there was a cushion between them, she could still feel his heat. And, strangely, being with him made her feel safe and protected. It had to be because he was so big, he made a great barrier between her and the world.

'Part of the reason I'm here is to provide additional security for Thadie,' Angus said, leaning his forearms on his thighs. 'According to my people, Thadie originally required a personal protection officer as an attention deterrent, not because she believed she was in danger.'

'I wasn't,' she agreed. Weeks ago, she'd just wanted the press and the public to keep their distance and Greg had done a good job keeping them away.

'The situation has changed,' Angus continued, looking at her. 'I don't like what happened today. The press mob was out of control and some of the comments on social media go beyond nasty and into scary. And weird. Occasionally, stalkers decide to take their fantasies into the real world. I believe you need additional officers until the worst of this attention blows over. Of course, it doesn't help that your ex-fiancé keeps giving TV interviews and stoking the fire.'

Thadie had left both voice and text messages begging Clyde to stop giving interviews and posting on social media. But she knew he wouldn't because Alta was in damage-control mode. When Clyde reminded people to look at her unhinged video, he garnered support. And he needed public support if he was going to salvage his multimillion sponsorship deal.

'He's not going to stop,' Micah said, before she could. 'Not unless we pay him off and pay him enough to make him go away.'

'He's not getting anything from us,' Thadie insisted. 'I'll admit that doing that press conference in my nightgown was stupid, impulsive and that it was good TV. But I would rather live under house arrest for the rest of the year than give him any money.'

'That's all very well, Thadie,' Micah pointed out, 'but the rest of us can't live in our houses too. Dodi has to be able to run her business, and Jago and I would like to be able to move freely as well, without having microphones and cameras in our faces.'

Thadie rubbed her arms around her waist, feeling selfish and mortified. She would be able to handle this conversation, and her brothers, a lot better if Angus weren't sitting on the couch, listening to every word. She lifted her shoulders to her ears.

'Then I really don't know what to do,' she reluctantly admitted.

Angus picked up her coffee cup, handed it to her and told her to drink. While she wasn't in the habit of blithely obeying anybody's commands, she did as he asked.

'The best solution would be to leave,' Angus suggested. 'Treat the press as you would a stroppy toddler. Remove the object of their attention.'

Thadie sent him a quick look. His use of the word 'toddler' was surely a coincidence. He couldn't know about the twins, could he? She knew that she had to tell him, but right now wasn't that time. There were other things to figure out. Including her own feelings about her twins' father coming back into her life.

She looked for evidence of their presence but, luckily, her cleaning service had been in earlier and had returned all the boys' toys to the playroom. Ten minutes after they returned to the house, this room would look as if a bomb had hit it. Gus and Finn had her brothers' messy genes.

Looking around now, she noticed how cold the house looked, a little denuded. She and Clyde had agreed to keep her furniture but she'd taken her artwork off the walls, thinking that her new husband should have a say in what went up there. She'd wanted him to feel at home in her house.

All her photographs of the twins were being reframed into matching, stylish black and white frames, as per Clyde's request for uniformity. She must remember to cancel that order and put her mix and match frames back up.

But only when Angus was back on the other side of the world…

'Thadie should leave the city, preferably the country,' Angus said. 'Two weeks should do the trick, but a month away would be a lot better. Go to New York, to the south of France. I hear that London is nice this time of year.'

What was he insinuating? Was she reading too much into that innocuous comment?

'London with the tw—'

'I agree that leaving is a good idea,' Thadie interrupted Micah, desperate to keep the twins a secret. At least a little longer.

Micah caught her eye and she frowned at him, offering him an infinitesimal shake of her head. She only hoped he and Jago picked up on her reluctance to tell Angus about the twins. Micah returned her frown and she realised thankfully he'd received her message. She looked at Jago, who was also regarding her with a piercing stare. She'd have to deal with their questions but, for now, she was safe.

'I like Docherty's idea,' Jago said, nodding.

Thadie admitted that, on the surface, it sounded like a good plan. But Angus had no idea that taking the twins on a vacation required planning and a second set of hands. She was a hands-on mum but trying to hustle two energetic twins through airports was a nightmare. Long car journeys were even worse. She'd do it if she had to, but it wasn't fun.

Micah, always in tune with her, sent her a sympathetic smile. 'What if we all disappear for a few days? Why don't we take a family holiday? You booked Petit Frère for your honeymoon. I instructed our booking agents not to take any other bookings for the next ten days. We could fly out tomorrow and return on Sunday, and Thadie could stay longer if she needed to.

'Apart from a small staff crew, the island is empty,' Micah explained, turning to Angus. 'Petit Frère is a small, exclusive resort on an island we own in Seychelles. The island has four villas, each separated from the other, as well as a small two-bedroom cottage. There's a central building housing the communal restaurant and bar, pool, gym and sauna.'

'Access?' Angus asked, his expression impassive.

'People can only get there by boat,' Jago replied, sounding enthusiastic. 'I think going to Petit Frère is a great idea.'

Micah flashed her a smile. 'It's simply a matter of calling our pilot, getting him to file a flight plan and getting Jabu to pack our bags. He'll insist on coming along to look after us.'

'Jabu?' Angus asked.

'Our semi-retired butler,' Jago answered him.

Thadie always felt uncomfortable calling Jabu by his official title. 'He's so much more than that,' she told Angus. 'He started at Hadleigh House when Jago and Micah were little, before I was even born. Jabu was the first person to see me walk, he taught me Zulu, because my mother wouldn't teach me the language. He's been my guide to my African ancestry.'

'He's more of a father than a butler,' Micah agreed.

'Anyway, getting back to taking an island holiday,' Thadie said, uncomfortable with the I-can-see-through-you gaze Angus was giving her. 'I think going away together, Jabu included, is a great idea and I would love it if we can make that happen.'

'When should we leave?' Micah asked. 'Tomorrow morning okay?'

Thadie nodded enthusiastically. 'Fine by me.' She turned to face Angus again. 'Since I'm going to be out of the country, I won't need additional security. But thank you for your concern,' she added, wincing at her formal tone. She needed him to leave. Needed some space to collect her thoughts and decide how she was going to tell him about Gus and Finn.

Angus stood up and put his hands on his hips. 'You're not getting rid of me that easily,' he rumbled in his water-over-gravel voice.

'I can't think of anything else we have to discuss,' she told him, lifting her nose. She hoped he didn't pick up on the fact she was lying.

'You *can't*?' said Angus, sounding intense. 'I can think of a couple of things…'

He turned to Micah and Jago, his smile cool

and composed. 'If you would excuse us, Thadie and I need to talk privately. It's nothing that concerns her security.'

Or you. Thadie heard his silent subtext and did not doubt that Jago and Micah did too. Jago looked at her, his eyebrows raised. 'Do you want us to stay?'

Absolutely not!

Thadie shook her head, her braids bouncing violently. 'No, it's fine. He's right...we need to talk. I'll call you later.'

Her brothers stood up, kissed her cheek, and walked out of her front door. Thadie suppressed the urge to run after them.

She waited until she heard the slam of their car door and sighed. She turned back to Angus and straightened her shoulders. 'What did you want to discuss?'

Angus's hot look pinned her feet to the floor, and she felt like a bug under a microscope. 'I want to return to my earlier question. I want to know why you didn't contact me, given our chemistry. You said you would, and I don't think you are a woman who goes back on your word. So why didn't you call me or send me an email?'

There was something different to Angus's tone this time. Something Thadie couldn't quite put her finger on.

She started to explain but he spoke right over

her. 'But, mostly, I want to know why you didn't tell me about them.'

He pulled a photograph from his back pocket and Thadie gasped, going hot and cold. She recognised the photo as one she'd pinned to the fridge months ago. Gus and Finn had put their plastic-moulded motorbikes in their bubble bath and were sitting on them, laughing like loons. The photo had always lived on the fridge, along with takeout menus and magnets and, honestly, she'd forgotten it was there.

Angus had not only noticed the photo but had managed to remove and pocketed it without her or her brothers noticing. Impressive in a slightly James Bond, scary, superspy way.

Her secret was out.

CHAPTER FOUR

'YES, THEY ARE YOURS.'

What else could she say? She'd wanted time to think, and this wasn't the way she wanted to impart the news, but she wasn't going to lie to him.

'Were you going to tell me? Or would you let me go back to London, oblivious to the fact that I am a father?' Thadie heard the anger in his voice, and she didn't blame him. She would be angry too.

Feeling as if she were holding onto a frayed rope, Thadie walked to the kitchen area of her all-in-one room and yanked open the door to the cabinet next to the fridge. She banged two glasses onto the counter and reached for a bottle of whiskey she kept behind the cookie jar. She poured them both a healthy slug, thinking that they needed it. It wasn't every day that you heard you were a father...

Or that you came face to face with the father of your twins. Thadie handed him a glass, knocked her shot back and looked longingly at the whiskey bottle. No, she had to do this sober. Not that she was in the habit of using alcohol to get through life and its many ups and downs.

Thadie told him to take a seat on one of the barstools on the opposite side of the island and, when he did, she rested her elbows on the marble countertop and tried to rub away her headache with her fingertips. 'These past few days have been the craziest of my life,' she muttered, mostly to herself.

'Still waiting,' Angus told her.

Right, here goes. She forced herself to meet his eyes. 'I'm going to explain why I didn't contact you first. Let's get that out of the way.'

He nodded and she continued her explanation. 'I lost my phone, remember? After I left the hotel, I got a new one and it was operational immediately. I was in the store when I realised that I hadn't picked up your business card when I left my hotel room. I called the hotel, frantic, but they'd already cleaned the room. I asked them to look for it in the rubbish, they said they would. I pestered them all that day, I went back to the hotel, checked and rechecked the room and talked to the head housekeeper, but they never found it.'

She didn't tell him that she cried, on and off, for days.

To her surprise, Angus closed his eyes and released a long breath. His reaction suggested that her explanation was a relief, but she didn't have the faintest idea why. She shrugged away her curiosity and continued her explanation.

'Since I only knew your first name, I couldn't track you down. I figured it was just one of those things, we had a moment, and it was over. Eight weeks later, I realised I was pregnant.'

Angus sipped his whiskey, his expression impenetrable. 'They say that condoms are ninety-nine per cent effective,' he rumbled, pushing his fingers into his hair.

She hesitated, blushing. The sex they'd shared had been hot and all-consuming, and nothing like the tepid encounters she'd experienced before, and after, Angus. But they'd used protection, except for that one time. They said it only took once.

Judging by the way they'd almost blistered the paint on her kitchen walls earlier, that hot and all-consuming part hadn't changed.

He grimaced. 'I'm sorry.'

Shortly after meeting him, and had her brothers not walked into her house, she and Angus might be on round two. She couldn't think when he touched her, and she wouldn't be hypocritical by criticising him for his lack of control when she had none herself.

'It was a chance we both took. We knew the potential consequences. And I wouldn't change a thing. The twins are, no doubt, the best thing that ever happened to me.'

He looked past her to the fridge, as if looking for more proof of their existence. 'How old are they…exactly?'

'They turned three a couple of months ago,' she said.

'And what are their names?'

She looked down and closed one eye. 'The oldest, by five minutes, is Gus. His brother is Finn.'

He narrowed his eyes, suspicious. 'You named him after me?' he demanded. It didn't escape her attention that he didn't thank her, for creating a link between them and the father she didn't think they'd ever meet.

'I would've given Finn your second name, but I didn't know it.'

He winced and shook his head. 'It's Moncreiffe.'

'Ah, maybe not, then.'

'Look, I wanted simple English names for the boys, and I liked yours. It's not a big deal.'

His sceptical look told her he didn't believe her. 'Let's get back to the subject of my recently acquired set of sons,' he said.

He made it sound as if he'd just picked up

a new car or purchased a new watch. Or had been gifted a new pair of socks. Suddenly furious at his seeming lack of emotion, his focus on the facts, she poked his forearm with her finger. 'Let's get something straight right now—they are *my* sons. You might've provided the biological material, but my name is on the birth certificate, I have spent the last three years raising and loving them. They are *mine*, not yours!'

He couldn't possibly think that he could slide back into her life and become an insta-dad to the boys. It didn't work that way. 'You are going to go back to London, and I will stay here and raise my sons.'

He looked confused and a little shaken and she couldn't blame him.

'Look, I'm still trying to make sense of this. I never envisioned having kids. It's never been on my radar. I admit that I need time to process this but I'm not going to ignore the situation,' he told her. 'They are my responsibility. I'm not going to pretend they don't exist!'

'Why not?' she asked. 'I have enough money to provide everything they need... Medical, great schooling and, later, to pay for their university education. I don't need your money, and you live on the other side of the world. And, more importantly, I know nothing more about you than the fact that you are a good lover. I don't know you well enough to know whether you'd be a good father to them. That's all I want for them.'

But memories of that night in London rolled over her, as resolute as a rogue wave. He'd been an exceptional lover, but she also recalled him as being thoughtful and considerate. It had been cold, and he'd placed his jacket around her shoulders as they'd walked from the taxi to the hotel lobby. He'd asked her, a few times, how she was feeling, whether she was sure she wanted to make love. And at every stage of their love-making, her pleasure had been at the top of his agenda. When she'd lain in his arms, sated and awash with the after-effects of sensational sex, he'd pulled a sheet up over her shoulder to make sure she wasn't chilly and the next morning he'd fetched her coffee from the tray delivered by room service at the crack of dawn. He'd been thoughtful and considerate to a woman who'd been little more than a stranger. She sensed that was simply part of his make-up.

But it was a big leap between treating a lover well and being a good father. And while she was prepared to be disappointed—her parents had disappointed her all her life—she refused to let that happen to her boys.

'You stated you wanted a good father for the twins,' Angus said, frowning. 'And you don't seem to be cut up about being dumped. Did you decide to marry Strathern because you thought he'd be good for Gus and Finn?'

Her mouth dropped open and she just managed to stop her wince. How did he manage to put those puzzle pieces together so quickly? Was he some sort of boy genius? Man genius, she corrected. There was nothing boyish about Angus.

There was no way that she was going to tell him about her lifelong desire to have a family, to recreate what she'd never had as a child.

'Well?'

'Are you always this nosy?' she asked him.

'When I'm interested. Are you going to tell me?'

'No.'

'Fair enough.' Angus placed his big hands on the marble countertop, his expression thoughtful. When he looked up again, she noticed his determined expression. 'I want to meet the twins. I want to know them. I want them to know me.'

Thadie rubbed the back of her neck, panic crawling up her throat. This was too much, too soon. The twins had been through enough…they didn't need…no! She had to be honest, at least with herself. She was the one who'd needed more for them, who'd wanted them to be raised in an old-fashioned family.

The truth was that the boys, not having seen much of Clyde lately, weren't missing his lack of input at all. Nothing much had changed in their world.

Another truth was that seeing Angus again scared her, being around him felt as if she'd been jolted with a cattle prod. He made her feel, made her yearn. And burn. She wanted his hands on her, his mouth on hers, her legs around his hips as he slid inside her…

He made her feel out of control and buzzy, as if she were sitting on the edge of a rocket and shooting through the atmosphere, burning up. Unlike Clyde, who was consistently calm and laid-back, Angus was tough, hard and direct. She didn't think he possessed a volatile personality, but he made *her* feel volatile, and that was enough for her to keep her distance.

'I am not dropping another father on them so quickly, that would confuse them.' Besides, she needed time to get used to the idea. 'The best thing would be for you to go back to London. You could start talking to them via video-call, you can get to know them that way. For the first few weeks, or months, I'll introduce you as a friend of mine and, if you manage to build a rapport with them, I'll think about the next step. I won't have them disappointed by another man who says he wants to be their father and then isn't.'

'I'm not in the habit of disappointing people, Thadie.'

People said that but they inevitably did. It was better to expect disappointment and prepare for it rather than let it sideswipe you. She'd spent her childhood and teens thinking that, waiting for her parents to see her, to spend time with her, but they could never be bothered. It was better to not want or dream than to have her hopes raised and shattered. She'd been prepared to marry Clyde because she'd known she'd never feel more for him than she should, ask or expect more than for him to be a dad.

And despite his perfidy, his underhand sneakiness, his defection didn't hurt. She was mad at him, livid, but not hurt. Her kids hadn't been disappointed by him—neither had she—and that was all that mattered.

Angus's expression turned thoughtful. 'I understand, and appreciate, your wish to ease them into the situation. But I still want to meet them.'

'I'm flying to Petit Frère tomorrow,' Thadie pointed out. 'There's no time.'

'There's tonight,' he countered.

No! She wasn't ready, not yet. She needed time to think, to plan, to work out how she was going to handle Angus's reappearance in her life. 'No, not today.'

The edges of his mouth lifted in a smile as he cocked his head. 'I don't think you have a choice,' he said. 'There's a car pulling up the driveway.'

In London, around Angus, her world had narrowed to encompass only him, and it seemed as if it had happened again. So much so that she hadn't heard Jabu's noisy Land Rover—an ancient beast he loved and adored—pull up outside. Now that she was paying attention, she heard the slam of heavy doors and the high-pitched chatter of her boys as they ran through the front door and into the great room, dumping their small rucksacks on the hall bench.

'Mum! Mum, where are you?' Gus shouted, excitement in his high-pitched voice. What had they been up to?

'Use your eyes, Gus,' Finn said, in his slow and deliberate way. Her youngest son was incredibly observant and had immediately noticed Angus. Then again, since he'd stood up on their arrival, they couldn't miss the tall, muscular stranger in their home.

Jabu stepped into the room and his eyes darted between Angus and herself, as curious as the twins. 'Jago said you were home, so I thought

I'd save you a trip and deliver the monsters myself,' Jabu explained.

'Thanks, Mkulu,' Thadie replied in Zulu, as she always did. She wished she'd thought to call him and tell him she'd collect them from Hadleigh House. 'Have they been okay?'

Jabu did a mini eye-roll. 'These two are always okay. They are indestructible. Who's the guy?'

'A friend from my past. He's also the owner of the security company,' Thadie said, moving from the kitchen into the lounge. The boys hurled themselves at her and wrapped their arms around her thighs, each jostling for position. Over their heads, Thadie introduced the two men and watched them shake hands.

Then Jabu switched to English. 'So, we were at the library, and they were having a talk on nature.' He winced, just a little. 'It was aimed at eight-to-ten-year-olds, on the oddities in animals, and they insisted on staying to listen.'

That sounded like something the boys would enjoy.

'I hear we are all flying to Petit Frère tomorrow?'

Thadie blinked at Jabu's change of subject. 'Yes. It will be good for all of us to get away,' Thadie replied.

Jabu agreed, hugged the boys and told her he'd see her tomorrow. Thadie closed the door behind him, and her eyes darted from Angus's rough-hewn face to her babies. They both had his eyes, bright against their creamy, light brown skins. Finn, whose features were rougher than Gus's, looked the most like him.

Thadie took a deep breath. 'Guys, this is a friend of mine. His name is Angus Docherty.'

Their sweet faces lifted to inspect Angus, two sets of eyes alight with curiosity. 'You're tall,' Gus told him, in his let-no-thought-be-left-unspoken way.

'Your name is like Gus's,' Finn commented and Thadie stared at him, astounded. She couldn't believe he'd made the connection between Angus's name and his twin's. Finn sometimes frightened her with his big brain, and this was one of those times.

'Our names are a little alike,' he agreed. His voice sounded normal, but Thadie saw the strain in his eyes, the tension in his big shoulders. Acting normal in front of the twins had to be difficult but she appreciated him making the effort. 'And yes, I'm tall.'

'Uncle Micah says that we're going to be taller than him,' Gus boasted. 'Uncle Micah is very tall!'

'I'm sure you both will be big guys. So, I heard you went to the library. How was that?' Angus asked, surprising her by engaging with the boys. It was obvious he had no experience with kids, but he was trying.

Gus's eyes widened as he hopped from foot to foot in excitement. 'Did you know that there's a lizard that can shoot blood from its eyes?'

'I didn't,' Angus replied. 'What else did you learn?'

'Cockroaches can live for a week without their heads,' Finn replied. He looked bewildered. 'I want to know how.'

Thadie winced. The boys were at the age where anything gross fascinated them, and they were sure to recount every bit of new knowledge they'd heard.

She saw amusement in Angus's eyes. 'Maybe your mum could help you look that one up on the Internet,' he told Finn.

Great, Finn would now badger her until they did exactly that. She did not want, or need, to know anything about cockroaches!

Gus wiggled, excited. 'And moths, no…flutterbies…'

'Butterflies?' Angus suggested.

Gus nodded, his eyes wide, about to impart information of great importance. 'Flutterbies taste with their feet!'

At Angus's laughter—rich, dark and sexy enough to scatter goosebumps on her skin—the twins were off and running, demanding Angus inspect their playroom and help them build a fort from old blankets.

Well, he'd said that he wanted to get to know them...

The floor-to-ceiling doors leading onto the entertainment deck were open and Angus was grateful for the cooling breeze. Thadie was somewhere in the huge house, bathing and putting the boys to bed. He sat on the edge of her leather couch and stared down at the intricate patterns of the Persian carpet under his feet. He had survived SAS training, had been pinned under enemy fire, taking a damned bullet to his thigh...

But he had never felt this unsettled. This wasn't something he'd trained for, knew how to handle. He'd had a commanding officer instead of a father and he had no idea how to be a dad.

It was strange to think that his father could be an incredible commanding officer but a completely useless parent. His mother hadn't been great either, to be honest. But up until his mid-twenties, he'd made excuses for them, and told himself he was overreacting.

Then he'd got shot. While recovering he'd made the incredibly hard decision to leave the army, thinking that if he couldn't stay with his unit, being on the ground, then he wanted out.

He'd thought his dad would understand why: if he couldn't do what he most loved, he had to leave.

Instead of providing understanding and support, The General had verbally assaulted him and disparaged his feelings and fears. He'd been mocked and dismissed. Instead of supporting him, his mum had sided with The General, telling him his father knew best.

Getting shot hurt, but the people who were supposed to love him the most had eviscerated him. Up until then, he'd been leery of love and commitment, unimpressed by the concept, but their response and lack of support had resulted in him vowing to avoid all emotional ties and bonds. It was better, safer, and less messy.

He'd lost his family over a decade ago, but he'd gained two sons today. Holy hell. Angus looked at his trembling hands and swallowed, then swallowed again. He felt disorientated, as if the world had slid off its axis and was hurtling into space.

Meeting Thadie today had been tough. She packed a massive punch he hadn't expected, and hearing he was a dad had sent him off into unknown territory. He'd never envisioned being a dad but life, or fate, had decided otherwise.

Thoughts rushed into his mind, collided and blew up. A couple hung around.

Where did they go from here? How should he handle this news? And, hardest of all, did he want to be a dad and what type of father could he even be?

As a child, he'd yearned for love, playful attention, kind words, and laughter. He'd never got anything but criticism from either of his parents. By his mid-teens, his ambivalent feelings about love solidified after his mum backed up his dad's feelings about him leaving the army. That day, he'd started creating his own legacy, and had also started constructing sky-high emotional barriers. He kept his emotional distance from people, rationalising that if he never allowed anyone to get close, he couldn't be hurt again.

The decision to avoid love, in any form, was made. Emotions were unnecessary. Discipline, focus, and hard work were what he'd need if he was to create a legacy that had no connection to The General. He refused to be distracted by relationships, by friendships, by women.

Did that extend to children he'd never known he had? Being a father wasn't something Thadie expected from him. She was very happy for him to walk straight out of her and the twins' lives.

He could do that, he admitted. He had met the boys and it was obvious they had a good life and were happy, and well looked after. He could easily put a debit order on his account and send Thadie money for maintenance. He could, as she suggested, talk to the boys via video-calls when his schedule allowed. She was making it easy for him, he just had to walk out of the door.

But he couldn't, he didn't want to. They were his *sons*, dammit, they were Dochertys, and carried clan blood in their veins. He wasn't going to force them to be soldiers or have anything to do with military life, but he did want the twins to know their family history. He might not like his father, but he was a proud Scot.

But what did he know about being a father? He'd never had one, having been raised by a general and his aide-de-camp. He'd had little contact and nothing to do with kids, hell, he'd barely been allowed to be a bairn himself, and he did not know how to raise happy and healthy— emotionally and physically—boys.

And, even if he had the daft idea to take on twin boys, where would he find the time? Running Docherty Security took all his time, and it was hard enough trying to carve out time to take on the specialised missions he so loved. How would he fit the boys into his life? Could he be a dad who operated from the sidelines of their life? Would that be enough?

Would they, one day, question his involvement, his commitment? It was obvious that his sons were as smart as whips, especially Finn, and they'd sense if he didn't give fatherhood everything he had.

The risk of failure was high.

And Angus didn't fail. Ever.

Sometimes not failing meant weighing options, making a tactical retreat, and coming at a problem via the back or side door. Maybe he could be their 'friend' as Thadie suggested—he could still be involved in their lives.

Without the responsibility and the risk.

The problem was that he wasn't a guy who shirked responsibility and he wasn't risk averse. He was responsible for thousands of employees. But the decisions he made about them were intellectual, rational decisions. As for risk, he was the guy his government called when they needed someone to think out of the box, to take above-average chances. He could do both for his business and his country...

But neither entity involved his emotions or asked him to lay his heart on the line...

And that was what being a father was.

He didn't know if he could be what they needed, or deserved, but neither could he walk away. Rock, meet hard place.

And he hadn't even started to think of Thadie and how she'd fit into his life.

Angus sat up and leaned back, resting his head on the back of the couch. She'd disrupted his life four years ago and had done it again today. Back then, he'd thought they were going to have a four-day affair, instead she'd disappeared. He'd thought he'd come here to find out how, and why, he'd read her—and the situation—wrong, but instead he faced fatherhood and the uncomfortable knowledge that his attraction to her was ten times stronger.

Attraction? What a stupid word for the tumultuous emotions coursing through his body. He desired her, craved her, needed to see her naked again. And under the lust, curiosity bubbled.

He now understood why she hadn't contacted him—not his fault, or hers—but his initial questions were replaced by so many more...

Why did a woman, blessed with intelligence and wealth, choose to marry a man she didn't love? Yeah, she said it was to give the boys a father, but she had a close relationship with her brothers, with the older, dignified, Zulu man. There were men in the boys' lives, she didn't need to marry to give them role models.

From Docherty Security files, he'd learned her background. Shortly before they'd met in London, she'd graduated with an MA in Fashion Design, but he couldn't find any traces of her being employed. Had she gone straight from her masters into motherhood?

What else?

She had a massive social media following and was regarded to be an influencer, and she also was involved in a few charities. But neither of those were enough to fill hours in the day. She could afford to hire help to look after the twins so why hadn't she resumed her career? Fashion was, he recalled from their first conversation in London, something she loved. Look, he respected women who were stay-at-home mums, he'd heard it was one of the toughest gigs in the world, but he couldn't quite put Thadie into that box.

The truth was that he needed more time: time with her, time with the boys, time for him to get used to his new reality. Time to figure out the puzzle that was Thadie Le Roux.

And his suddenly overly complicated life.

Angus lifted his head as Thadie stepped into the room. She looked exhausted, her lovely skin tight across her cheekbones. He had been trained to adapt to new situations quickly and he was feeling the strain. After all that had happened to her over the past few days, and, as he'd heard, over the past few months, the rope holding her together was fraying. It was time to leave, to give her some space.

He stood up and walked over to the table in the hallway where he'd left his phone and car keys. He picked them up, slid his phone into the back pocket of his trousers and closed his fingers around his car fob.

'Get some sleep, Thadie,' he told her, resisting the urge to cuddle her close. She looked as if she desperately needed a hug, but, because he desperately wanted her, he couldn't trust himself not to take it further. Besides, he wasn't someone who knew how to hug. Or give comfort.

She walked past him to pull open the front door but stopped to place her forehead against the expensive wooden door. 'I wasn't going to ask you this, I promised myself I wouldn't, but I can't help myself,' she muttered, her voice so low that Angus had to step closer to hear her words.

He placed a hand on her shoulder, encouraging her to turn around. She folded her arms across her chest and stared down at the floor, her bottom lip caught between her bright white teeth.

'Ask me what, Thadie?'

She pushed the tips of the fingers of her right hand into her forehead, keeping her eyes closed. 'What you thought of the boys...'

In a blinding flash, he knew she wasn't asking whether he liked Gus and Finn—because he'd made it very clear that he did—but what he thought about her success as a mum. He cupped her cheek, using his thumb to gently lift her face, and told her to open her eyes and look at him. She looked apprehensive and insecure, and very annoyed she was looking for his approval. But he was more than happy to give it.

'They are wonderful kids, Thadie, bright and

confident. It's obvious that you are a wonderful mum,' he told her. His mother had been as cold as his dad had been tough, and approval—love and affection weren't something either of his parents knew how to show—had been linked to his achievements. That wasn't the case in this house...

'Good job, sweetheart,' he added.

He saw her swallow, then she nodded, and tension seeped from her body. Then her eyes turned darker, if that was at all possible, a deep, unfathomable coal black. Unable to pull his gaze away, he stroked her full bottom lip with the pad of his thumb. The air around them crackled with electricity, and his world narrowed, filled by the beautiful woman in front of him.

Don't touch her, just walk away. It had been a long, emotional, strange day, he shouldn't complicate it further by kissing her again. Then Thadie's tongue came out to touch his thumb and he was lost, pulled into a vortex of want and desire and red-hot need. He moved so that her body was between him and the door, so close that a piece of paper couldn't slide into the space between them. He was instantly, completely hard and straining the zip of his trousers. His mouth met hers, soft, sweet, spicy, and he had to fight his instinct to strip her of her dress, her underwear, take her up against the door in the most primal and passionate way possible.

Where was all this want and need coming from?

Thadie's arms encircled his waist and her hands skated up under his shirt, cool against his fevered skin. Needing more than her mouth, to touch the bare skin of her arms, and shoulders, he pulled down the thin strap to her dress and pushed his fingers under the lace of her bra, his fingers finding her nipple. She whimpered and made that low growl in her throat that he remembered so well. It was an I-want-you growl, a take-me-now sound.

He wanted to. She had *no* idea how much.

But she was feeling overwhelmed, and he didn't sleep with drunk-with-tiredness-or-emotion women. He never took advantage of a woman just to get a temporary physical high. When they slept together again, and they *would*, he wanted her to have no regrets...

He was known for his legendary willpower, but it took everything he had to pull his mouth off hers, his fingers off her breast. He rested his forehead against hers, listening to her ragged breaths.

'I should go,' he murmured, holding her hands next to her sides.

She nodded, her tongue touching her top lip, trying to recapture his taste. He resisted the sharp, insistent urge to kiss her again and take her to bed.

'You should,' she agreed, not sounding convinced. Tugging her hands from his, she put her hand on his right pec and pushed him back, creating some much-needed space between them. Thadie opened the front door, hauled in some fresh air, and stood back so that he could pass.

'Invite me to the island with you,' he said, verbalising the thought that had been rolling around in his head.

'What?'

'Invite me on your family holiday,' he said, watching as confusion jumped into her eyes and skittered across her face.

'Like your brothers, I can work remotely. I can take some time to get to know the boys. We could figure out a way to go forward that doesn't involve video-calling. We can get to know each other, become friends, and build trust.'

Thadie didn't look convinced. 'I don't know whether my brothers would appreciate having a stranger gatecrash their holiday…' she said, and Angus knew she was looking for a reason to say no.

Luckily, he had an answer for that. 'Technically, it's *your* honeymoon and you can invite whoever you want.' He saw her waver and pushed a little more. 'A little time, Thadie, that's all I'm asking for. Time for us to wrap our heads around being back in each other's lives and for me to connect, in some way, with the sons I never knew I had.'

She stared out into the darkness beyond his car and held up her hand, asking for a moment to think. Angus pushed back his impatience. If pushed too hard, she might dig in her heels. After a few excruciatingly long seconds, she turned back to him and nodded, albeit reluctantly. 'I might come to regret this but…yes, okay.'

Angus wanted to punch the air but kept his hands in his pockets instead.

'But you can't tell anyone, not the boys or my brothers, Jabu…anyone…that you are the twins' father. As I told them, you're an old friend. I've invited you along to keep me company so that my brothers could spend some alone time with their fiancées without them all worrying, and feeling guilty, about leaving me alone.'

Whatever reason worked, as long as he was achieving his objective. 'Deal. At the end of the holiday, we'll have another conversation about the boys and how to tell them.'

'*If* I tell them,' she quickly corrected him.

He shook his head and the truth hit him, knocking him off his emotional feet. He didn't know how to be a dad, how to protect his heart, but he was not going to give up his sons, for any reason. Yes, he was terrified he'd make the same mistakes as his father, but he couldn't get anywhere if he didn't *try*. Winning the fight was impossible if you didn't step into the ring.

It was that simple. And that convoluted.

'Let's get something straight, Thadie. They are my sons, and they *will* know that I am their father. Maybe not right now, but some time soon. Start wrapping your head around that.' He bent his head to kiss her temple, inhaling her scent again. 'I'll call you in the morning, early, for details about when we depart and from where. But get some sleep, you look shattered.'

'I am,' she agreed, sounding cross. 'And your unannounced arrival didn't help.'

'We'll sort it out,' he said, not knowing whether he was trying to reassure her or himself. 'We're smart people, we can find a way to be friends, lovers and raise our kids without any drama. I don't do drama.' Not giving her a chance to reply, he stepped onto the path and walked towards his car, moving swiftly.

He was half inside his car when she twigged. 'We're not going to be lovers, Docherty!'

Oh, yes, they were. That was the only thing he was sure of. He glanced back to see her standing in the doorway, the light behind her highlighting her many curves. Gorgeous. 'Want to bet?' he asked, before sliding into his car and shutting the door.

She'd lose money if she did.

CHAPTER FIVE

THADIE TIPPED HER face up to the hot sun and released a long breath, thankful to be in the powerful speedboat on their way to the island. They'd spent the morning travelling—flying with the twins on her brothers' private plane was so much easier than flying commercial—and they would arrive at Petit Frère in five or so minutes, in time for a late afternoon swim and to watch what would be a stunning sunset.

Thadie opened her eyes to check on the boys, decked out in their small life vests, sitting between Jabu and Micah, bouncing with excitement.

Her eyes—hidden by the lenses of her very dark sunglasses—skipped over her family and fell on Angus, his nut-brown hair blowing in the wind. The wind plastered his white button-down shirt against his wide chest, reminding her of his chest and stomach muscles. Beneath his rolled-up-to-his-elbows sleeves, his forearms were tanned, the hair on his arms bleached by the sun. His easy-to-wear shorts ended above his knees and his legs were tanned too.

Could she be blamed for her insane attraction to him? The man was incredibly, deliciously hot.

Enough of that, Thadie, pull yourself together!

It had been another strange day, starting with sending her brothers a message telling them Angus would join them, explaining that he was accompanying her to Seychelles as her friend, and as extra protection in case the press followed them to the island. But, thankfully and for the first time ever, they kept their comments to themselves, shook his hand and welcomed him on board their private jet. The twins bumped the fist he held out and Finn even gave him a shy smile.

She couldn't tell her family, not yet, that Angus was the twins' father. For all she knew, they might've guessed. But she was still wrapping her head around the idea of him meeting Gus and Finn, being in her life, and wasn't ready to discuss anything with anybody. And she had no idea how to answer the questions she knew they'd ask: would he see the boys? Would they take his name? Pay maintenance? What role would he play in their lives?

She didn't know and until she did she'd keep everything under wraps. Until she was ready to explain, Angus was a friend she'd recently re-discovered.

Angus leaned forward so that his words wouldn't fly away with the wind. 'Can you orientate me?'

Thadie looked around, easily identifying verdant islands popping up from the flat blue sea. Her father had negotiated a lease from the Seychelles government the year she turned eighteen, and she'd been visiting Petit Frère for twelve years. In the beginning, there were just a couple of houses but when her brothers inherited his business, they developed the island into a super-elite, exclusive resort that guaranteed luxury.

'We're north-east of La Digue, and north-north-west of Felicite Island. The island is south-west of Petite Soeur,' Thadie explained. The speedboat did a long turn and Thadie knew they were close to Petit Frère. Two minutes later, they entered the bay and Thadie pointed to the beach. 'There's the pier.'

The boat slowed to an idle and approached the long pier. A wooden pathway started at the bottom of the pier stairs, crossed the white sand beach and zigzagged up a hill. It ended, as Thadie knew, at the entertainment area, with its huge pool, sprawling lounge, bar and open-air kitchen. Micah hopped off the boat to tie it down and the twins bounded to their feet. As her family stepped off the speedboat, Angus joined her and, without asking, helped Finn to unclip his life vest, and she bent down to help Gus. He looked at the clear water and back at the twins.

'Can they swim?' he asked, worried.

Thadie nodded, pleased he was thinking about their safety. 'Like fish,' she replied. Then she shrugged. 'But, obviously, they aren't allowed to go near water without an adult.'

The twins dumped their life vests and scrambled off the boat. After Angus picked up the vests and handed them to the skipper, who took them down below, he turned to Thadie and captured her hand, giving it a quick squeeze. 'Are you okay?'

She thought about giving him a breezy answer but shrugged instead. 'I didn't sleep much last night. It's been a stressful few days.'

In the space of four days, she'd been dumped, caused a scene in front of the press, been mobbed and been reunited with her never-forgotten lover and her son's father. It was a lot to cope with and maybe that was why she responded to Angus the way she did. Her world had been rocked, she'd felt battered and bruised and his kisses made her forget her name.

And everything else.

He pushed his hand through his hair, remorse on his face. 'You might not believe me, but I never intended to place more stress on you. I just want to spend some time with my sons and find a way to move forward that works for all of us.'

He placed his back to the pier, creating a solid barrier between her and her family, keeping his voice low so that only she could hear his words. Unfortunately, when he lowered his voice like that, it turned deeper and sexier, like rich velvet sliding over her skin. His fresh cologne took on a hint of sea and Thadie pushed her knees together when she felt that low, warm hum between her legs.

She turned away and looked out to sea.

Pleading exhaustion on the flight to Seychelles, she'd handed the twins over to her family and disappeared into the plane's bedroom. Instead of sleeping she'd spent the five hours of flight time examining the craziness of the past few days, specifically her immediate, fire-hot reaction when Angus kissed her. Part of it was a sexual hangover from London—she'd felt young again, unencumbered. Angus was someone she found attractive, always had, and probably always would. When he kissed her, everything—the kids, her disastrous non-wedding, the responsibilities of life—disappeared and it was lovely to just *feel*.

But she knew she had to corral her attraction to him, had to get it under control because, even without his connection to the twins, it was far too soon for her to consider jumping into bed with another man. She needed to find her emotional feet again, to be on her own and to figure out exactly what she wanted. Her last attempt to create the family had backfired horrendously.

Angus wasn't the answer to her prayers, nor was he the man she needed to make her family complete. And—this was a thought that popped into her head at the beginning of the flight and wouldn't go away—maybe, just maybe, her family was perfect the way it was, with just the three of them. Her boys had Micah and Jago, and Jabu as role models and they were fine men. Yes, being a single mum was tough, but she'd survived the hardest years. She had plenty of money and her family's support...

Maybe she'd been looking for something she thought she needed but didn't. Not really. And how stupid did that make her feel?

Yes, Angus made her yearn and burn, but that was attraction, desire, a biological need for sex. She had to look at him clearly, look at their situation without rose-coloured glasses. He was the twins' dad, not a potential love interest. She wasn't ready for another relationship, not until she sorted her head out.

'I don't want to cause you more stress, Thadie,' Angus told her when she turned to face him again, his thumb stroking the inside of her wrist. 'But something is bubbling between us, we both know it.'

'And it's complicated by the fact that you are Gus and Finn's father,' Thadie agreed.

He pushed her sunglasses onto the top of his head and frowned. 'Look on the bright side— with my arrival you don't have to think about marrying to give the twins a father. I am their father so you can stop looking for another one. That's the real reason you agreed to marry your ex, right?'

'I...' she spluttered, caught off guard. She started to deny it but stopped. It was the truth.

'How did you work that out?'

Angus stuck his thumb out. 'Reason number one, when you were doing that impromptu press conference—gorgeous dressing gown, by the way—' Thadie glared at him but he ignored her '—you were angry, but you weren't hurt. Your pride has taken a beating, but your heart is intact.'

Accurate but she wasn't about to tell him that, so she remained silent.

'And, two, you would never kiss me like you did if you were still in love with another guy. I remember you checking, and double-checking, whether I was single back in London. You don't cheat, physically or emotionally. And if you still had any feelings for your ex, there's no way you would've inhaled me the way you did yesterday.'

'I think you are overstating my reaction,' Thadie told him, heat in her cheeks. He wasn't but he didn't need to know that.

He folded his arms, completely at ease in the rocking boat. 'I don't think I am. So, am I right?'

He was, but Thadie had no intention of making his head swell any bigger by confirming his suspicions. She rolled her eyes and stepped from the boat onto the pier, turning back to look at him. He looked amazing, sunlight creating gold flecks in his dark hair. He was far too sure of himself, and, worse, of her. She looked at her family, who were using the narrow wooden path to cross the hot white sand. The twins had, naturally, stepped off the deck and were running on the sand, playing tag. Her beautiful boys...

Their beautiful boys. Hers, his, theirs...

Thadie felt her vision narrow and she swayed on her feet. She was emotionally and physically exhausted and the stress and anxiety of the past few days were waiting in the wings, ready to ambush her. She felt like a wet rag that had been wrung out and left to dry. She felt the deck coming up to meet her, but a pair of strong arms held her upright and gently lowered her to sit on the deck. Angus told her to bend her legs and pushed her head between her knees, his big hand sliding under her braids to hold her neck.

'Breathe, Thadie, deeply and evenly. When last did you eat?' he demanded, his voice rough.

She thought about it and shrugged. She'd had an apple for breakfast and refused lunch. Too hyped up by Angus's unexpected arrival in her life, she hadn't eaten any supper last night.

'No food, stress, exhaustion, twin boys and a long-ish flight east will do that to you,' Angus told her, balancing on the balls of his feet next to her. She turned her head to look at him and her heart banged against her ribs at the worry she saw in his eyes. It had been a long time since a man looked at her as if he wanted to take on the world for her.

Angus's hand moved from her neck to her shoulder. 'Better?'

She nodded.

He stood up and hauled her to her feet, lifting his hand to run it over her head, his knuckles drifting down the side of her face. His eyes darkened with determination. 'Right, here's the plan. You're going to eat great food, sleep late, lie in the sun and chill. Your only job is to relax and unwind.'

That sounded like heaven. 'In case you didn't notice, I have two whirlwinds to keep lassoed,' she told him.

'I'll keep them entertained,' Angus told her. 'Give me some ground rules and I'll take over.'

She lifted her eyebrows. 'Um… I don't think that's the best idea you've ever had.'

He threw his hands up in the air, at the doubt he saw on her face. 'I was a lieutenant in the SAS, Thadie, and I led men into battle. Don't you trust me to keep them safe?'

'I do,' Thadie quickly assured him, instinctively knowing he wouldn't let them come to any harm. But he had no idea how exhausting the twins could be, with their constant questions and their six-in-the-morning to seven-at-night energy. They simply never stopped. Angus had no idea what he was taking on.

'Then let me look after them for you,' he insisted. 'I can get to know them at the same time.'

Oh, he was going to get to know them, very well indeed. She gave him a day, maybe two. He might be a Special Forces soldier but dealing with Gus and Finn required a set of skills not taught in the military. But she wasn't sending them to another island, she'd be in shouting distance. And the best way to learn to be a father was to *be* a father. He'd be tossed into the deep end, and it would be a good way for him to learn whether he wanted to do this for the rest of his life.

She shrugged. 'Okay.'

Angus looked as if he'd won a victory. 'Really? Awesome! It'll be fun,' he stated, rubbing his hands together.

Fun? Occasionally. But it sure would be relentless.

On Friday afternoon, shortly before lunch, Thadie stepped into the entertainment area, and gratefully accepted the offer of an iced coffee from the hovering waiter. It was another hot bright afternoon, and she wore a brightly patterned sarong over a lime-green bikini.

Her non-wedding, the viral video and Johannesburg felt a long, long way away. She also felt a hundred times better than she did when she almost fainted on the pier on Wednesday afternoon. Had it been the day before yesterday? It felt like a week, maybe more.

Thadie looked down to the beach, her eyes on Angus, who sat on the sand next to where the boys were building sandcastles, his tablet resting on his knee.

She'd known many good-looking guys in her life, but Angus was the only one to ignite a flame in her belly, between her legs. His features weren't perfectly symmetrical, his nose was a little long, his chin a too strong but no one noticed because he was so intensely, utterly masculine. With his wide shoulders, his big arms and muscled legs, he exuded power. And even better, control of that power.

He was, in every way, the most alpha of alpha males. And she knew of what she spoke, her brothers were good examples of the species. But Angus seemed to have something extra, an undefinable quality that made him stand out...

Maybe it was his stillness, his complete confidence in himself. He'd been an exceptional soldier in one of the best military units in the world, and he'd fought in wars. He'd survived. Maybe that gave him the edge, that extra boost of confidence.

Whatever it was, it was as sexy as hell.

Two days had passed since her come-to-the-light thoughts on the plane. She felt rested, less stressed and a great deal more relaxed. And, hour by hour, day by day, she was far more accepting of being a single mum. Her kids were happy, and confident—had she needed to sacrifice her happiness and freedom?

Angus's arrival in her life, him being their real dad and wanting to be involved in their lives, had also removed any pressure she might feel to repeat her give-them-a-father fiasco. He was their dad...she never had to worry about that again.

Yay.

Thadie's thought was interrupted by a big hand on her back. She smiled at Micha as he joined her at the railing, and placed her temple on his shoulder, happy to lean into him, as she did when she was a little girl. And as a big girl.

Micah pointed the rim of his beer bottle in Angus's direction. 'You've got a billionaire owner of an international security company working as your au pair. You're *good*, shrimp.'

Thadie lifted her head to look at him. 'He's that rich?'

Micah nodded. 'Oh, yeah. Angus's company is as big as, maybe bigger than ours, and he's a very hands-on CEO. I don't know how he does it. Jago and I have enough to do but he does it solo. But, somehow, the man also makes time to take two or three holidays a year, and he goes off the grid and is unavailable. We want to know how he does it.'

Holidays? Why didn't that sound right to her? She couldn't imagine Angus sitting on a beach, drinking a cocktail. Or sleeping late before hitting a couple of ski slopes. That didn't gel. He seemed too busy, too focused, and too into control to leave his business for long periods and not be contactable.

Micah's information had to be faulty.

Or was she making excuses for him, or only paying attention to what she wanted to see? She'd done that with Clyde and made a mess of her life. Maybe she should learn from that lesson.

'He's an impressive guy,' Micah commented.

Yes, he was. Everything, from his gorgeous body to his masculine face, deep voice and sharp mind enthralled her about Angus. And that was why she had to be extra-careful to not let her libido override her intuition and common sense.

'He's also, currently, the most expensive child-minder in the world,' Micah said, his voice filled with laughter. 'Which raises the question…why *is* he looking after the monsters? We're grateful he's keeping them occupied but one has to wonder why.'

She felt his eyes on her face and knew that if she looked at him, he'd read the truth in her eyes. She suspected they all knew Angus was the twins' dad—how could they not?—but she wasn't ready to confirm it. Or even talk about it. 'He's a friend who wanted to give me a break.'

'Yeah, right,' Micah scoffed. 'That's not why.'

Thadie was thinking of a way to answer him when a scuffle broke out between Gus and Finn, involving a spade and bucket. There was another spade and bucket, but no, they both wanted to use the blue one. Thadie watched as Angus placed his hands on his knees and stared at the sand, obviously looking for patience. Yep, she got it, she frequently felt like that herself.

'I'm actually feeling sorry for the guy,' Micah said. 'He's been with them pretty much constantly since we arrived.'

Thadie pulled a face, feeling guilty. 'I know. I think it's time for me to take them back.' She sent Micah an impish grin. 'But, damn, it's been nice.'

He smiled back, before taking a sip of beer. 'Jago and I are going to look at another island, about thirteen nautical miles from here. It's available to be leased. We want to see if it's suitable for development into a resort like this one. If we leave this afternoon, we can take the boys. We'll be back tomorrow afternoon.'

'How will you feed them? Bath them? Where will they sleep?' Thadie demanded.

Micah rolled his eyes at her. 'Jabu is coming along too, along with a couple of staff members who'll set up the tents and cook for us.'

Thadie smiled at him. 'Ah, you're glamping...'

Micah grinned. 'Yeah. Anyway, we'll barbecue on the beach tonight, the kids will love it. It'll be an adventure.'

'Dodi and Ella?'

'They are staying here. They both want a quiet evening.'

Thadie looked over to Jago, who was reading his book, one hand resting on Dodi's baby bump.

'You're really good with the twins, Micah, but we both know Jago finds them overwhelming.'

'They *are* overwhelming but he's having a baby soon and he needs practice,' Micah told her, his voice firm. He nodded at Angus. 'And he needs a break.'

'And maybe,' Micah added, tapping his beer bottle on his thigh, 'by the time we come back you could give us the truth why Angus gate-crashed our family holiday?'

Maybe, Thadie thought as he walked away. But probably not.

CHAPTER SIX

ANGUS STEPPED ONTO the deck of the villa—the building was bookended by two huge granite rocks—and walked over to where Thadie sat by the pool, her book in her lap.

The twins had left in a flurry of excitement, and Angus watched the two powerful speedboats—one driven by Jago and containing Micah, his boys and Jabu and the other containing two Petit Frère staff members, and their food and equipment—disappear around the side of the island. Then he showered and sat at the desk in the study to pick up his emails. He'd expected to skim through his work—Heath could make most of the day-to-day decisions—but it was nearly an hour and a half before he joined Thadie on the deck, carrying a beer in one hand and the icy mojito he'd whipped up in the other.

He handed her the big glass and sat down on the lounger next to her.

'Peace,' he muttered, stretching out his long

legs and closing his eyes. He opened one to look at Thadie, who still wore her brightly patterned sarong over her bright green bikini. She'd pulled her blonde braids into a high tail and, because she wore no make-up, he could count the dainty freckles on her cheeks and nose.

Despite being at Gus and Finn's command for the last forty-eight hours—he now knew SAS training wasn't as demanding as looking after those two—he'd spent a lot of his time watching her and he more than liked what he saw. Oh, she was stunning, and she heated his blood, but there was more to her than her long body and gorgeous face. She was an attentive mother, fully present. She was also a very sexy woman, someone who had no idea of the impact she made.

'Are you regretting your offer to look after the boys?' Thadie asked, amusement in her voice. He had to force himself to stop imagining how she'd taste with the mint-and-rum drink flavouring her mouth. Fantastic, he had no doubt.

He looked at her, her sexy lips wrapped around the straw of her drink. 'Regretting it? No. Just recovering…'

'There are rather full-on, aren't they?' Thadie grinned.

'I can easily cope with the physicality required, running up and down the beach, swimming, kicking a ball around,' Angus answered.

'It's the questions that threw me. Why is the sky blue? How many grains of sand are on the beach? How do birds stay up in the air? And my favourite…what does food think when we eat it? I mean, how am I supposed to answer that?'

Thadie's laugh sounded like a spring racing over baby rocks. 'My favourite is still whether God likes marshmallows.'

'Finn,' Angus stated, thinking that question could only come from his more serious son.

'Finn,' Thadie agreed. The look she sent him made him feel ten feet tall. 'How did you know that? You've spent so little time with them, but you seem to have sussed them out. Clyde knew them for nearly a year, but he still mixed up their names.'

The boys looked alike but they weren't identical. Their differences were easy to spot. And the more he heard about her ex, the more he wanted to rearrange his face. But he was out of her and the boys' life, so there was no point in discussing the waste of oxygen.

'You're good with them, Angus,' Thadie told him. 'And thank you for giving me a break. I needed it.'

'I know.'

It would be so easy to take her mouth in a hot kiss, to slide his hands over her, but he didn't want to push, didn't want to spoil this moment of connection between them. They'd get there, very soon, but for the next few minutes, he just wanted to bask in the warmth of her eyes and enjoy the softness of her smile.

Besides, the anticipation was awesome.

Angus forced his gaze off her face and looked at the ocean, thinking of his boys being on the boat with Jago and Micah. He'd personally put them into their life vests, and had watched them speed out of sight, fighting the urge to call them back.

'Will they be okay with your brothers?' he asked, despite knowing that Thadie would never let them go if she weren't fully confident that they'd be safe.

'They will be absolutely fine. Micah is even more protective of them than I am, and that's saying something,' Thadie replied, putting her glass down on the side table that separated their loungers. 'Dodi is my best friend, but Micah was who I called at three in the morning when I was at the end of my rope. He's been there for them, and me.'

Thadie half turned to face him, the nail polish on her bare toes shimmering in the sunlight. Pretty. Then again, everything about her was.

'Did you have any help apart from Micah? Did you employ a nanny? Do you have an au pair?' Angus asked, curious about her life.

Thadie shook her head and he saw her jaw tighten and her lips flatten. He'd hit a nerve and didn't know why. 'No, just me,' she answered.

He frowned, trying to make sense of her answer. 'You don't work?'

Thadie's eyes sparkled with annoyance. 'My father left me a lot of money and I chose to stay home and raise the boys. Do you have a problem with that?'

He lifted his hands, wondering at the flash of her temper. 'Of course I don't, I'm just trying to understand.'

Thadie sipped at her mojito before resting the back of her head on the lounger. She tucked her legs up under her butt and released a long sigh. 'Sorry for snapping, it's a touchy subject.'

He wondered why but knew this wasn't the right time to ask for an explanation. They'd get around to it...

Now, or later, but it would happen.

'You've done a stunning job with them, Thads, they are great kids,' Angus told her, needing her to know how much respect he had for her. 'Thank you.'

Thadie smiled at him, her irritation melting away. 'Someone once said that one's greatest achievement might not be what you did but who you raised. I hold onto that.'

Angus heard the note of longing in her voice.

Did she want to do something else, something for herself, or was his imagination working overtime? If he pushed her for an answer, she might shut down and they'd be mired in awkward, tense silence. No, he most definitely didn't want that.

'I think you're raising Finn to become the president of the world.'

Thadie's smile was as powerful as an asteroid strike. 'Nope, Gus will talk his way into that role, and Finn will be the power behind the throne.'

Accurate, Angus decided.

He caught her eyes skidding off his thighs and hid his smile. He'd noticed her looking at his stomach, his arms, her dark eyes gliding over his chest. She'd been checking him out and she liked what she saw. 'So, we have a decision to make,' he said, flicking his finger against his beer bottle.

Thadie looked at her mojito, shook her head and sent him a pleading look. 'Angus, the kids have just left, it's blissfully quiet and I have a lovely drink in my hand. I know that we need to talk about the boys and your role in their life, but can we postpone it, just for a little while?'

Ah, yeah, he'd thought she'd jump to that inaccurate conclusion. He wanted something else, and he was pretty sure she did too. There was only one way to find out.

'I was only going to ask you whether I could take you to bed.'

It was a bald statement, no frills, but Angus didn't see the point in dancing around the subject. He wanted her, more than he wanted his heart to keep beating, but he now knew she wanted him too.

Thadie sent him a what-on-earth look and her drink sloshed in her glass. He removed it from her grip, placed it on the table between them and raised his head, his eyes slamming into hers.

'I want you, Thadie. Desperately.' He pushed his hand through his hair and released a laugh that was short on amusement. 'From the moment I picked you up and carried you to my car, I've thought of nothing else.'

Thadie placed her hand on her heart, half covering the breast he so desperately wanted to kiss.

Her eyes darted to his mouth, and he saw her swallow, once and then again. 'I... Angus...' She closed her eyes, pulled in a deep breath and when she spoke, her words rushed out, like a spring tide racing to the shore. 'We've always had a crazy attraction, a hot as hell chemistry.'

That wasn't a yes. 'But?'

'But this isn't London and we're not who we were,' she insisted, looking both terrified and earnest. 'It's so much more complicated this time around. The boys...'

It shouldn't be. 'The boys and how I am going to be in their life is a separate conversation, Thadie. They have nothing to do with the fact that I look at you and my mouth goes dry and the blood drains from my head. Seeing you in your gorgeous bikinis and not being able to touch you has sent my blood pressure rocketing.

'I want you, you want me,' Angus added. 'Let's make that happen.'

She was on the verge of agreeing but something held her back, a hesitation that wouldn't let her slide into his arms. 'You make it sound so easy!'

'It is easy,' he replied, keeping his voice low and even.

She lifted her hand, her palm facing him. 'Hang on, hotshot. Let me catch my breath.'

Angus forced himself to back off and gave her some time to think. When she spoke again, she sounded a little less breathless.

Damn. Still so sexy.

'I've got to think about this, Angus. I was engaged to another guy less than a week ago.'

'He made you angry, but he didn't break your heart and you're not emotionally vulnerable,' Angus calmly reminded her. 'You're single, Thadie, and if you want to have a one-night stand or a dozen of them, that's your right. I'd like you to have one, or a couple, with me.'

'So straightforward, Docherty,' Thadie murmured. 'No hearts or flowers or fancy words.'

He'd never been and never would be the type. 'Not my thing,' he assured her.

Thadie cocked her head at him, her gaze direct. 'So, I'll be another one-night stand? Is that what you are after?'

He hesitated but before he could answer her, she was off again. 'I mean… I don't, necessarily, have a problem with that. I'm not ready for another relationship, or anything really! I'm just trying to see things as they are, not as I want them to be.'

'Can you explain that?' Angus asked.

She shrugged. 'I didn't look at my relationship with my ex closely enough. I imagined it to be better than it was. If I'd been thinking clearly, if I'd asked more questions, I might've realised that he was behind the efforts to sabotage the wedding. I thought that because he was laid-back, he wasn't ambitious. He was calm but I failed to see how sneaky he was. If I'd asked more questions, probed a bit more, was more present, I could've avoided a lot of grief and wasted money.'

'So, now you're asking questions?' he clarified.

She nodded and shrugged. 'Now I'm asking questions.'

Fair enough. He considered giving her a flip answer but that wasn't fair. The very least he could be was honest. She deserved that and giving her half-truths, as her ex had, would be insulting. And he wasn't that type of guy.

But how did he tell her that, having been rejected by his parents, and used as a pawn by his father, he was terrified of emotional engagement? He was trying with Gus and Finn and opening up to them was hard enough. Falling in love, allowing someone to take possession of his heart? He still couldn't see that happening. How could he give someone who professed to love him—someone he wanted to love and please—the power to treat his heart like a bowling ball and dictate the terms of that life?

But he had to tell her something. And it had to be the truth.

'I've never been married, engaged, nor have I had a long-term partner. I like living my life solo, having no one to answer to. I'm not good at relationships,' he told her, holding her gaze. 'I have affairs, Thadie, that's as emotionally deep as I'll go. I'd like to have one with you, for as long as that works for both of us.'

'Okay, well, that was blunt.'

He couldn't read the emotion in her eyes and that frustrated him. Was she relieved? Or disappointed? Damn, where were his reading-the-room skills when he needed them?

Did she need reassurance? And if she did, what could he tell her? That he'd change for her? That because she fascinated him, he'd allow the chains wrapping his locked-away heart to fall away and he'd take a chance on having a relationship with her? But, given his upbringing and dismal interpersonal skills, he would fail at giving her what she needed, and he'd hurt her—and himself—in that futile quest.

He didn't fail and, since he knew he would fail at being what Thadie needed, he wouldn't even try.

But there was one thing they were spectacular at: they had a chemistry that was extraordinary and exceptional...

'I can make you feel good, Thads, better than before,' he said. 'Let me take you to bed, where I'll make you forget all the chaos of the last few months and remind you of what it is to feel sexy. Feminine, powerful. Wanted beyond all meaning.'

He saw the capitulation in her eyes, the need to be in his arms. He lifted one eyebrow. 'Yes?' he prompted.

'Yes.'

Thank God and all his angels and arch angels. Picking up her hands, Angus tugged her to him so that her lips were an inch from his. 'Too much talking,' he murmured. 'Definitely not enough kissing.'

'I agree,' she replied, her sweet breath fluttering against his lips.

'Slide your thigh over mine,' he told her.

'Why?' Thadie asked but did as he requested.

'So that you'll be more comfortable when I do this…' Angus said before slanting his mouth over hers, tracing the seam of her lips with his tongue.

She tasted like the woman he'd met before, as an awesome memory should. But this kiss was tinged with something different, it was deeper and darker and more intense than he remembered. Thadie felt like the upgraded, full version of the woman with whom he'd spent the night in London, richer and far more interesting than he expected. She felt amazing, soft and luscious and so very feminine.

Falling into the kiss, she placed her bikini-covered core on the hardest part of him and pushed down, creating friction. His eyes rolled back in his head at the slap of pleasure as he welcomed her weight, one arm encircling her butt to hold her tight against him, letting them burn. His other hand held her jaw, his fingers tracing her sharp cheekbone as his mouth ravaged hers.

Thadie hooked her arm around his neck and

pushed her breasts into his pecs, dragging her Lycra-covered nipples across his bare chest. He deepened the kiss, needing to taste her, to delve, to dip and dive, needing to explore every part of her mouth. Heat and lust ricocheted through him and, for the first time in four years, he felt his body sag, his bones melt.

Angry ninjas, machine-gun-toting Special Force soldiers and aliens could land right next to him but nothing would stop him from kissing Thadie, from exploring her satin-and-silk skin, her curves, tasting the honey between her legs, the dip of her spine.

He pulled his mouth off hers so that he could speak. 'Bed, *please*.' It was only two words but there was no way he could make complete sentences, as all his blood had left his brain.

Thadie hesitated, wrinkling her nose. She couldn't be second-guessing this, could she?

'Be with me for the rest of the time on Petit Frère,' he suggested, his voice hoarse. It was all he could give her. 'Share my bed, Thadie, let me worship your body.'

She started to speak, hesitated and bit her lip. 'Nobody can know,' she told him. 'I don't want to answer awkward questions from the twins, from my brothers and Jabu. We're lovers when we are alone, friends when we are not.'

Angus felt a momentary pang of disquiet

and pushed back his urge to claim her in public. There was nothing more between them but intense chemistry and the twins. And, as he'd stated, those were two very different entities.

'This can't affect any decisions about the boys, and our way forward, it's just sex,' Thadie insisted, her fingers still dancing over his abs. 'It's just between us.'

He nodded, his hands sliding up her long thighs. Annoyed by the barrier of her sarong, he yanked it off and dropped it to the floor. It fell over her book and Angus remembered that they were outside and could be interrupted by Dodi and Ella, both of whom were still on the island. Swinging his legs off the lounger, he stood up, Thadie in his arms and carried her into the house, and into his bedroom, to lay her down on the white cotton duvet.

She looked, he thought, as if she belonged there.

It was a temporary thing, Angus told himself, a flame that needed to burn out, a rogue wave that needed to slap the shore to expend all its energy. It wouldn't last...

It couldn't.

Angus's suite was off to the side of the house and from his private, inaccessible deck, there was an endless view of the sea. But her attention wasn't on the stunning view or the way the afternoon sun danced across the mirror-like water. No, all her attention was focused on the big, intense man standing at the end of the bed, looking down at her, drinking her in. Thadie took in his tall frame, and his messy hair. His black board shorts hung low off his hips, and she licked her lips at his exposed, superhot hip muscles His skin was tanned gold from his hours in the sun. Brown scruff covered his jaw, and his bare feet were surprisingly elegant. She wanted to take big, greedy bites out of him…

Oh, she was in so much trouble, teetering on the verge of losing control.

This was about sex, about taking what she offered…a way to feel sexy again, feminine, wanted and wonderful. It had never been this good with anyone else, not even close. But she couldn't overthink this, get carried away. This wasn't anything more than unbelievably good sex. He was a gift to herself, a lovely distraction. She'd had some awful months and Angus was giving her a way to forget—great sex with no caveats—and she'd take it…

Thadie knelt on the bed and placed her hands on his rough jaw and moved to align her mouth with his. His hands tightened on her hips, and then his lips were under hers. Lust and need made the air between them shimmer, and she caught a glimpse of golden sunbeams as her tongue slipped between his open lips and into his mouth. He tasted like beer-flavoured sin. How had she lived for four years without feeling so alive? *Had* she lived?

He allowed her a minute to explore his mouth before taking control of their kiss. He wound a strong arm around her waist, pulling her up against his chest—hard with muscle. He kissed her with skill and confidence, as if he knew what she needed and how to give it to her. Overwhelmed by sensation, Thadie slumped in his arms, but Angus just tightened his grip on her.

'I've got you.' He pulled back to murmur the words against her open mouth. He hesitated, shrugged and dipped down again, and dialled up the kiss from hot to insane.

Angus painted kisses across her shoulders and Thadie inhaled his fresh sun, sea, and hot-man scent, the heat from his body engulfing her. Her nipples puckered against the triangles of her bikini and she swallowed, noticing there was no moisture left in her mouth. He was plastered against her, and being in his bedroom—a beautifully decorated space dominated by this huge bed—felt incredibly intimate. She felt as if she belonged there, that being in his arms was where she needed to be.

No, she was doing it again, reading more into

a situation than there was. This was just sex and if she was going to become mushy, then she should roll away and put some distance between them until she regained a modicum of control.

His hand settled over her breast and Thadie knew she was fooling herself, she had no intention of applying the brakes to stop this runaway train. Her tongue twisted around his, and she arched her back to press her nipple into his palm. She was putty in his hands…

Thadie murmured her appreciation when his thumb brushed her nipple, her soul smiled when he pulled at the strings at the back of her neck. Her bikini fell down and, with another tug, her top gave way and Angus tossed it to the floor. He lowered his head to take her nipple between his lips, his fingers skimming over her stomach and ribcage. His tongue moved to her other nipple, sipping and sucking and rediscovering her.

Thadie's hand skated across his body, exploring the defined muscles of his back, the width of those impressive shoulders, and the strength in his big arms. He was so powerful, intensely masculine. While she liked what he was doing to her breasts, she didn't like the small space between them, needing every inch of her body to be connected to his.

Preferably naked…with him inside her.

Angus kissed her jaw, the spot beneath her

ear, and raked his teeth across her collarbone, finding all those long-neglected places craving his touch. Suddenly she was a glorious combination of fire and lust and want, a kaleidoscope of energy that started and ended with him. A part of her—the teeny-tiny inch of her that wasn't desperate for an orgasm—fretted over how incredibly attuned they were to each other. Still. They knew how to touch each other, to ratchet up the pleasure.

They knew each other, even better than before. How?

Angus picked her up and laid her across the bed and bent down to suck her nipple. She sighed when his teeth scraped over her and whimpered when he moved his mouth across her breast to her sternum and licked his way down to her stomach. Angus dropped to his knees on the floor and gripped her hips, pulling her to the edge of the bed. He knelt between her thighs, his hands gripping her hips, his thumbs on her mound. Needing more, Thadie lifted her hips, silently demanding that he *do* something. Angus inserted his finger into the side seam of her bikini bottoms and traced her thin strip of hair.

'Is this what you want, sweetheart?'

She couldn't talk, only feel. When no words hit her tongue, Angus spoke again. 'Thads, do you want me? Want this?'

'Please don't stop,' she begged, half sitting up to press his hand against her and opening her legs wider to give him complete access to her. She cried with pleasure when his finger stroked her, exploring her folds and slipping inside her.

'You are so very beautiful,' Angus murmured. 'So responsive.'

'Come inside me, Angus. I need you.'

'I need a condom,' he told her, turning away to pull open a bedside drawer. She caught a glimpse of the foil packet he tossed on the bed, wanting to weep with relief.

Angus surged to his feet, his hands going to the drawstring of his board shorts. Thadie pushed his hands aside and pulled the cords apart, pulling open the Velcro fastening. Pushing her hand under the fabric, she found his hard length, thinking that, like every other part of his body, he was stunningly, ferociously masculine.

His board shorts fell to the floor and Angus stood between her falling-off-the-bed legs, his eyes glittering, his cheeks flushed. He pulled her bikini bottoms down her thighs, slid on the condom and pushed against her entrance, hard and delightful. Thadie dug her nails into his firm buttocks, pulled him forward and Angus sank in an inch. His eyes slammed closed and Thadie knew he was fighting for control, fighting the urge to plunder. To conquer. To take.

But she wanted him unhinged, out of control because she wanted him to feel the way she did. She launched her torso up, hooked her arms around his neck, and looked into his bright blue-green eyes. 'Take me, Angus, fill me. And do it *now*.'

His lips quirked up at her bossy comment and he punished her by holding back, slowing his hands down and keeping his mouth an inch from hers. Yeah, he gave the orders, he didn't like taking them.

'Think you can keep that up, soldier?' Thadie teased him.

Without giving him time to answer, Thadie lifted her hips in a fluid movement, and he slid inside her.

Angus's eyes narrowed. 'That was…unexpected,' he muttered.

She didn't want to talk, she needed action. She wanted to feel overwhelmed, swept away… completed.

'Stop talking, Docherty,' Thadie murmured, lifting her mouth to meet his. He kissed her deeply, his tongue echoing his skilled movements down below. Thadie was on the verge of shattering when Angus's mouth turned tender. He slid his hand under her butt, lifted and tilted her hips and Thadie felt him even deeper inside her.

Exquisite sensation slapped her sideways and she tumbled willingly into a bright kaleidoscope, dancing among the colours. As she tumbled through reds and greens and purples, yellow and golds, she heard Angus's shout, felt his body tense and his release, wondering if he was seeing, feeling, the colours as she was.

She hoped he was. Like him, it was too good an experience to miss.

CHAPTER SEVEN

THE SUNSET THAT evening was magnificent, a riot of pinks, purples, gold and orange, the sky tossing colours into the sky to say goodnight to the sun. Thadie watched the colours change and the sea turn an inky blue. The stars started to pierce the sky and, sitting here, she felt like a well-loved woman, and not like a harried mum. This was who she was when she took the time to be herself.

Despite her six-month engagement to Clyde, it had been four years since she'd rolled around a bed with a sexy man, feeling reckless and free. The infrequent sex she'd shared with her ex had been uninspired. But she hadn't questioned it.

She hadn't questioned much.

She'd thought that snagging a father for her boys was all that mattered.

But that wasn't true, not any more. What she wanted and needed counted too. It was hard to admit but she'd neglected herself, and her needs, over the past few years. Her parents had never put her first—she didn't think she'd even made the list of their priorities—so she had done the opposite and given everything she had, and more, to her sons. In trying to balance the scales of her past, she'd swung in the opposite extreme. And it only took being dumped an hour before her wedding, meeting her ex, forty-eight hours to recover, and two rounds of spectacular sex to come to that conclusion.

She definitely needed to be quicker on the uptake. But she was trying, and that counted too.

They'd meandered down to the beach for a swim after making love a second time, holding hands as they walked down the path, arms around each other as they crossed the sand. After swimming out to the reef, they fooled around in the shallows, exchanging long, unhurried, luxurious kisses. Standing in the sea and enjoying the warm water on their bodies, Thadie wrapped her legs around Angus's hips and leaned back into his loose grip.

She tipped her head back, looking at Rock Villa nestled into the shadows of the granite rocks, the colours of the sunset bouncing off the huge windows.

'It feels like we're the only two people on the island,' she said, her thumb brushing over his collarbone.

'It does,' Angus agreed, his eyes turning greener as the sun dipped lower. 'Are you sure no one is expecting you to join them for a drink or a meal?'

Thadie shook her head. 'Both Dodi and Ella said that they wanted an evening alone.'

'Excellent news,' Angus said, his hand covering her breast and his thumb swiping her nipple. 'I like being alone with you, sweetheart.'

Thadie saw the desire in his eyes and slowly kissed his mouth, falling into that space where nothing else existed, just him and her and a spectacular barrage of colours in the sky. Scared of the feelings rolling and rollicking inside her, she pulled away and pulled her hand across the surface of the flat sea. *Take it down a notch, Le Roux.*

'You've met everyone important in my life— tell me about your family.'

Angus looked down at Thadie, caught off guard by the change of subject. He rarely spoke about his parents, and since he'd left the army few people made the connection between him and his father. He liked it that way, liked not being compared. But Thadie wasn't just another acquaintance, and she had the right to know more than most.

'My father is a general in the British Military, some would call him a legend. Colm Docherty?'

Thadie shrugged. 'Sorry, my knowledge of military generals is lacking.'

Angus walked her into the shallows and then onto the sand. 'Let's sit,' he suggested.

Thadie sat, the waves lapping their toes, her shoulder pressing into his.

'My dad is an army guy, through and through. So were my grandfather, and great-grandfather. Each generation has climbed further up the chain of command than the one before,' Angus explained.

'You were in the army, right?'

He hesitated and he hoped it was too dark for her to notice. 'I served,' he said. 'It was expected of me. I found out that I liked it, and I went on to join the SAS.'

'They are the badasses, right?'

He smiled. Yeah, they were. 'I loved being part of the unit. I reached the rank of lieutenant but over the next few years, I refused further offers of promotion. I didn't want to sit behind a desk. I wanted to be with my guys, at the coalface. My father was not happy.'

He couldn't believe that he was opening up, that the words were rolling out of him, a strange and unusual occurrence.

'And by not happy I take it you mean that he was furious?' Thadie asked.

'Incandescently. He wanted me to shoot up the chain of command—being constantly promoted was what Dochertys did but I wanted to stay where I was, with my team,' Angus stared out over the endless blue ocean, barely taking in the now dark island in the distance. In daylight, it shimmered with various shades of verdant green.

This was so far from everything he knew and was familiar with. His office in London, his cold flat, the missions he undertook. And without warning, instead of the perfumed island air, he could smell the dust of the village, instead of the heat of the sun, he felt the heat of a rocket exploding in a building behind him.

He hadn't had a flashback in years.

Thadie's hand on his thigh, small but strong, pulled him back to the present. 'Are you okay? You lost all colour in your face and your breathing started to hitch.'

Freaking marvellous.

'Sorry, a memory steamrolled over me,' he admitted.

Thadie's eyebrows raised. 'Of?'

He sighed and pulled up the hem of his shorts to show her the ugly scar. 'My unit was in a firefight. I caught a bullet in my thigh, and I was evacuated out.'

She stared down at his leg. 'I've always wondered how that happened. Can I touch it?'

He wanted to tell her that there wasn't a place on his body off-limits to her, but nodded instead.

'I'm so sorry,' Thadie whispered, her long finger tracing the scar. Most women recoiled from the puckered skin, white and red in places, the ridges and dents, but Thadie touched it as if she were trying to absorb any residual pain. He watched her finger, fascinated and turned on. She lifted her eyes to meet his and he saw the warmth and empathy in hers. Thank God, because he couldn't stand sympathy or, worse, pity. He'd never told anyone what came next...

'My father came to visit me in hospital, the day after my last operation,' Angus said, capturing her hand and holding it against his thigh. 'He didn't ask me how I was, whether I'd walk again, anything to do with my injury or about the incident. He had clearance, he could've asked me anything about that skirmish, but he didn't.'

He couldn't look at her but concentrated on a crab scuttling across the sand and into the foam at the water's edge. 'All my father said was that I was up for promotion again and that if it took me nearly losing my leg to finally get me moving up the chain of command, he'd take it. Two of my best friends died in that ambush and he would've known that!'

Thadie's eyes shimmered with emotion. 'That's so awful, Angus.'

'At that moment I realised that I wasn't a son to him, but a pawn to move about as he saw fit. I told him that if I couldn't stay with my unit, and I couldn't, I was leaving the army. He told me I was staying where I was. How he thought he'd keep me there against his will, goodness only knows. We had a shouting match in the hospital ward. I resigned the next day and within a year Docherty Security was up and running. And making money.'

A small frown puckered Thadie's forehead. 'And that's important to you?'

He shrugged. 'No, not particularly. But I like the fact that it irritates and annoys my father that I can afford things he can't.'

'I suppose every man wants enough money to do the things they enjoy. To be able to provide for his family. To spoil his wife.'

Angus's low laugh held no amusement. 'Not The General. No, he had a series of mistresses and he spoiled them, as much as he could.'

Thadie winced. 'How long have you known about his extra-marital affairs?'

'My dad introduced me to the first one when

I was thirteen. His dalliances weren't kept a secret, even from my mum.'

'Ouch, that's young. I was in my late teens when I realised that my parents were unfaithful,' Thadie admitted.

Angus snorted. 'My father wouldn't have tolerated my mother having an affair. She's his property, under his command.'

'Do you still have contact with him? Your mum?'

He shook his head. 'No. In my weaker moments I reached out twice, but gave up when they didn't return my calls or respond to my emails.'

Fury bounced into Thadie's eyes. 'Charming,' she muttered, and Angus knew she was holding back harsh criticism. Angus felt one or two of the icy chains encircling his heart snap. She was fully Team Angus.

He'd let her step into his inner world but now he didn't know what to do with her, where she should go. And that was more terrifying than storming a terrorist stronghold, walking straight into enemy fire. This was uncharted territory in every sense of the word.

And because she made him feel too much, threatened to snap those chains—they were industrial strength and, he thought, indestructible—and because he was floundering, he felt compelled to put some distance between them. This felt too intense, too real.

'I saw a bottle of champagne in the bar fridge. What if I run up and get it, and a couple of glasses?' he asked, jumping to his feet. He touched her bare shoulder. 'Are you cold? Do you want a towel or a T-shirt or something?'

Thadie sent him a gentle smile as if she understood why he needed to run. 'It's a lovely, still hot evening, Angus, I'm fine. But take all the time you need.'

Right, well…okay, then. He was obviously as transparent as glass.

Thadie watched Angus easily jogging up the steep path to the villa. She understood his need to be alone—she felt the same.

Like him, she needed a moment to find her bearings, to stabilise her ship, to breathe. Around Angus, she felt as if she were running out of air, her brain shut down and her body, and its needs, took over. She needed a few minutes to regroup.

To think.

She didn't regret making love to Angus. That had been inevitable. From the moment they'd met again, she'd known that being in his arms, in his bed, was just a matter of time. She might be totally addicted to the way he made her feel physically, but at least she wasn't confusing sexual chemistry with love.

Sex was sex and love was different. If they could keep the twins' relationship with Angus separate from their nuclear attraction, then she could do the same for her sexual urges and feelings.

It was just a matter of choosing her thoughts, and looking at the situation clearly.

She glanced towards the north-east, thinking of her boys on another island. Was she a bad mother for desperately wanting a few days, maybe more, to explore their chemistry and attraction? Time for them to talk, make love, be, without having a little person interrupting them, demanding something from her, whether it was a cuddle or a cookie, to be a referee or a reader.

Thadie bit her lip, feeling guilty at wanting Angus to herself, enjoying this time away from them. She'd be lying if she said she never relived their London night together, fantasised about being together like this. He was, after all, her hottest sexual encounter.

For the first time in four years, she felt free to be, wholly and authentically, herself, without reference to anyone else, including the twins.

But what would her life look like when they left the island, when Angus returned to London? Would every hour in the day be dedicated to the twins? Or could she carve out some time for herself by sending her kids to a morning-only playgroup or nursery school?

The thought immediately made her stomach clench and twist. She'd always been so hell-bent on doing everything herself. But, instead of dismissing the idea as she normally would, she decided to examine why she was beating herself up for wanting to do something for herself.

For the first few years of their lives, she was so conscious of being all the twins had and she'd been driven to do everything herself, to be a super-mum. Because if she didn't do absolutely everything herself, she would be like her parents, who'd never done anything at all.

Liyana had never changed a nappy, her father hadn't known what one was. They'd never lost sleep because she was crying, nor dealt with a childish temper tantrum. They'd simply employed nannies, then au pairs, to raise her.

Why be a parent when you could pay someone to do it for you?

Not wanting to think about her parents, she switched gears. It was, she decided, a good time for her to spread her wings. The twins were old enough to attend nursery school or a playgroup in the morning, and they would benefit from being around children their age. She could have the morning to work at…something. She could, for a few hours a day, be something other than a mum. And if she had a few hours free in the morning, maybe she could start designing fashion again.

The thought created little sparkles on her skin and her stomach rolled over in delight.

Truth was, she was jealous of those women who seemed to have it all, who effortlessly juggled the demands of a career with being a wife and a mum. They were, in her mind, superwomen. Thadie also envied Dodi and Ella. Her brothers' women supported themselves, and they did not need their fiancés'—or in her case, her father's—money. She also wanted to feel strong, capable, fulfilled…to be more than just the twins' mum.

Before she'd met Angus, before she'd seen those two lines on that pregnancy test, she'd had plans and had burned with ambition. All her life she'd watched her brothers' meteoric rise to be two of the continent's most influential businessmen, and, while she had no desire to be a captain of industry, she'd vowed to make her mark in the world of fashion.

Le Rouxs, as her father had always said, did not hide their lights under a bushel. She'd graduated top of her class and had secured an internship to work under Bryce Coin, who was now the creative force behind Quills, one of the

newest and most creative fashion houses in the
world. But all that had come to a screeching stop
when she'd realised she was pregnant.

Maybe there was a path back to that…

But along with excitement, she felt fear, dark
and harsh, swamping her tentative plans. What
if she found amazing success, loved it too much
and got involved in her career, in her new life,
and started to neglect her sons? What if she
wasn't successful at all? What if she stepped
back and Angus stepped up and he became their
primary caregiver, the person they turned to because she was too involved in her interests, her
life?

What if she forgot that the twins were the
focus of her life?

No, she'd never do that to them. She knew
how much it hurt to have selfish parents. Her
boys would always be her highest priority.

Thadie felt Angus kiss her shoulder before he
settled behind her, legs on either side of hers.
'You're miles away, Thads. Please tell me that
you don't have any regrets?'

She rested the back of her head on his collarbone as the purple colours in the sunset deepened to indigo. 'Not about what we did, no,' she
told him.

He pulled back from her and changed position
so that he could see her face. He bent his long

legs, rested his wrists on his knees and looked at her, curiosity in his eyes. 'What do you regret, Thadie?'

She pulled a finger through the fine white sand, wondering whether he would understand her sudden second thoughts about her life, her choices to be a stay-at-home mum, her frustration at never quite feeling she measured up. Like her brothers, Angus had never let anything stand in his way. Then again, none of them had found themselves single and pregnant with twins.

'Do you ever come face to face with yourself, not sure whether you like what you see?' Thadie asked.

'I like what I see,' Angus murmured, picking up her hand and placing a hot kiss in the centre. He dropped her hand and held it against his thigh. 'What don't you like, Thads?'

And there was the sixty-million-dollar question. 'Sometimes I feel dissatisfied and unfulfilled. I've been feeling like that for a while, and I thought it was because my wedding plans were going awry because Clyde and I were drifting apart.'

'But it wasn't that,' Angus said, conviction in his voice.

She nodded. 'No, I've realised it goes deeper than that. I was, am, unsatisfied about…well, me.'

'Why? You're incredible!' His astonishment

made her smile and fed oxygen to the ever-persistent flames of desire. 'You're sexy and stunning and you're such an amazing mum.'

Look, she loved hearing that she was a good mother but once, just once, she'd also like to be told she was smart and successful. 'That's the thing, Angus—people only see me as a good mum.'

'You work for charity, and you have this enormous following on social media, promoting body positivity,' Angus argued.

'I work for various charities, but that barely takes up any of my time. And, let's be honest, they like having me sit on the board, and attending their cocktail parties and balls, because I'm a Le Roux. As for the social media following, this idea that I'm a body-positive influencer is nonsense. Of course, I believe in the concept, but I was only tagged with that label because I frequently publish posts encouraging new mums to give themselves a break about their post-baby weight,' Thadie countered.

'Being a mum is hard enough without having to look as good as you did before you had kids. The last thing new mums need is to get caught up in the unless-we're-skinny-we-can't-be-happy nonsense,' Thadie added, feeling fierce.

'Being healthy is what's most important,' Angus agreed. He reached for the bottle of champagne he'd carried to the beach, along with two glasses, and pulled the tag to remove the foil. 'But we're getting distracted. Tell me why you feel dissatisfied.'

Thadie watched as he popped the cork and poured pale gold champagne into crystal flutes.

'I was a pretty good fashion designer once,' she explained. 'I was offered an internship with a famous designer.'

'What happened?' Angus asked. She simply looked at him, her eyebrows raised. He pulled a face, catching on quickly. 'You discovered you were pregnant.'

Thadie sipped at her champagne. 'Yeah. I wanted to keep working, but my brothers didn't want me in New York on my own. And then I heard that I was having twins and was expected to work twelve-to-sixteen-hour days. I knew it wasn't feasible.'

Angus rubbed the back of his neck. 'So you lost the opportunity,' he stated.

'Yep,' she agreed. 'I helped Dodi out in her bridal salon until I got too big to move, and after the twins arrived, looking after them took up all of my time.'

Angus rested the base of his glass on his knee. 'We touched on this earlier, but I'll ask again… Why didn't you hire someone to help you? I mean, you're not short of cash.'

'I had a nanny growing up—I had a *series* of nannies. My parents handed me over to whomever they could hire to look after me and I swore I would never do that to my kids. My parents didn't hear my first word, didn't see my first steps. I didn't want to miss a thing the boys did, so I knew I had to be actively involved.'

'You had to be the mum you never had,' Angus murmured. He lifted his glass to his lips, all his attention on her. When Angus listened, he really listened. Thadie knew he was taking in her every expression, listening for a change in emotion, on high alert for subtext. Like earlier, when he'd been making love to her, he paid attention.

'We both won the Horrible Parents Lottery,' Angus stated.

They had. Thadie turned her head to place a kiss on the ball of his bare shoulder.

Angus's eyes slammed into hers and her lungs stopped at the determination she saw in them. 'I don't want to be that sort of parent, Thads. I want to break that cycle and be an amazing dad. And I need you to teach me.'

She stared at him, confused.

'I need you to show me how to be interested and involved, supportive and how to communicate. You make it look so easy.'

Thadie felt tears burn her eyes. Being told that

she was a wonderful mum was a wonderful compliment and a sure way to melt her heart. Best of all, she knew Angus was being totally sincere.

'Thank you. They just need to know that you are there, that you are a soft place for them to fall,' Thadie told him.

They sat in silence as the sun disappeared behind the horizon, enjoying the purple-indigo light, waves sliding up and slipping down the beach.

Thadie broke the silence. 'I'm thinking about sending them to nursery school. And I'll need to find a way to fill those hours when they are at school.

'Yes, we're a very wealthy family and my father was a terrible dad, but he had a work ethic like no one else I've ever met. My brothers have worked their tails off to get where they are, Dodi and Ella are also incredibly hard-working. We work, we don't sit at home painting and doing pottery, going to the gym.'

She waved her hands in the hair, wincing. 'That sounds judgemental. I'm not trying to insult stay-at-home mums. I've been one for three years! If that's your thing—it's been mine—and you can afford it, who am I to judge? But I'm a Le Roux and I'm not made to live off the inheritance I received. I mean, I could, but *I* don't want to!

'You should see Dodi's face when she's found the perfect dress for a bride or after she's paid out staff bonuses—she's happy and proud and she feels so fulfilled, like what she's doing *matters*. Ella feels the same way when she's pulled off an incredible event, the same way my brothers feel when they close a complicated deal,' she explained.

'The way I feel when I execute a successful mission,' Angus murmured.

Mission? That had to be Angus-speak for picking up a new client, Thadie decided. He was retired from the military, he couldn't be involved in anything dangerous any more. He was a CEO now, not a soldier. So why did she feel as if there was something he wasn't telling her, as if he was holding out on her?

Angus topped up her champagne glass and Thadie looked at it, surprised. When had she finished the first glass? She didn't know.

'So, what's the plan?'

Thadie shrugged, confused. 'For what?'

'For you to start feeling fulfilled, Thads. What do you need to do for that to happen?'

Her lower jaw dropped. She was shocked at his understanding and immediate support. 'Uh... um... I don't know, I need to think about it some more. I need to decide what's best for the boys.'

'What's best for the boys is that they go to

nursery. I absolutely support you on that. Kids need social interaction. They learn more from their peers than they do at home,' Angus firmly stated. 'And, if you need more time in the day, then they can either go to an after-school programme or we can hire an au pair.'

Thadie felt instantly overwhelmed. She was just starting to work things out for herself, to plan a new life, and she didn't need him stomping in with his size thirteens and taking over. 'Whoa, hold on...*no*! No after-school programme and no au pair...that's not happening.'

Angus placed his hand on her knee and squeezed. 'Many kids grow up as children of working mothers and they are just fine. I grew up with an unhappy stay-at-home mum and, trust me, that wasn't fun. If *you* are happy, the twins will be happy. So, when I come back, I think we should visit schools, see if they can take them immediately. I can ask my PA to set up an appointment. We'll go together. Actually, that might be best because my schedule can change rapidly.'

This was all going too fast. It was too much. She hadn't thought things through with Clyde. She hadn't examined her motives or her decisions. She wasn't going to do that again, to be pliable. And weak.

She wasn't prepared to make another mistake

because she was being swept away by a man who mentally, emotionally and physically rocked her world. Angus made her feel off kilter and, worse, hopeful.

Okay, she wasn't in this raising-kids-alone situation any more. She could bounce ideas off Angus and there was someone else to take responsibility. She could, maybe, lean on and rely on him...

But what if she did that and he decided, in a week, or a month, or a year, that fatherhood wasn't for him, and she was left alone, pushed aside again? She'd stood on the outside of her parents' lives growing up, and they'd disappointed her time and time again. Clyde had made her promises he'd had no intention of fulfilling and she was terrified that Angus would do the same. Scared that, one day, she'd look around and he wouldn't be there...

And because she loathed feeling scared, hated the fact that he'd given her a taste of hope—because she was sliding back into old patterns of behaviour—she lashed out.

'You've been their father for a few days, Angus, and you're presuming to tell me what to do and how to do it? Just because you're suddenly enamoured with the idea of being a father, does not give you equal rights here! They are my children, my responsibility, and I will make the decisions, not you.'

She saw her words land like missiles, detonating in his eyes. Hurt chased anger across his face before his expression turned remote and unemotional. 'I was only trying to help, Thadie,' he said, standing up and brushing the sand from his shorts.

She scrambled to her feet, the dam wall holding back her emotional floodwaters crumbling. 'Where were you when they couldn't pick up one of their heartbeats? When they were both screaming and I didn't have enough milk and I didn't know if I could do this for one more second?' she shouted, slapping her hands onto his chest. 'You weren't there. I went through that all by myself. And you don't get to swan in like a white knight now.'

Thadie felt him grip her hands, and she tugged them away to wipe the moisture off her cheeks, frustrated by her tears. She was mad, not sad. He had no *right*…and she was stupid to feel tempted to let him into her life.

Angus stepped back and held up his hands, his expression as remote as a Siberian outpost in January. He started to speak but shook his head. He bent down, picked up the glasses and tossed the remains of the champagne onto the sand. He picked up the champagne bottle and, without looking at her again, walked away.

Thadie closed her eyes, frustrated at herself and the situation. She wasn't handling this well, she really wasn't. Just when she thought she knew what she was doing, and where she was going, life threw another curveball at her. She clenched her fists, and stared at her bare, sand-covered toes, waves of embarrassment and frustration rolling over her. This was what it felt like to stand on a leaky raft in the middle of a tempest, cold and scared and not knowing where she was going or how she was going to get there.

After a few steps, Angus stopped, turned and his eyes lasered through her. 'I'm deeply sorry I wasn't there for you, that I missed the first three years of their life. But I can't change that because I didn't *know they existed*. But I'm standing here, offering to share the load. You can either make this easy on us and find a way to work with me, or we can fight about this, and make both our lives miserable. But understand this, I will be a part of their lives. I am *not* going away.'

She wished she could believe him, but a person didn't need to physically disappear to make her feel abandoned. 'At some point in my teens, I realised I felt lonelier when my parents were around than I did when they were away. I won't let you do that to the boys,' she stated, unable to look at him.

He didn't reply and when she looked up to see if he had left, her eyes slammed into his, and even in the low light she could see his anger and frustration. 'I thought we agreed that we are going to be better than our parents. And, please, just be honest about why you are pushing me away.'

'What do you mean by that?' Thadie cried.

'You're not worried about me swanning in and out of the boys' lives, about the effect on them. You're terrified of our incredible attraction, the crazy chemistry, and you're trying to protect yourself. Just like I am. Fair enough. But blaming me for not being there? That's bloody insulting.'

With that conversational hand grenade, Angus stepped off the beach onto the wooden, slatted path and started to make his way back to the house.

Well, that hadn't been the way she'd expected this night to end. And she had no one to blame but herself.

Angus stood on the pier and watched the sleek speedboat approach from the north, Jago at the wheel. The twins, his boys, were seated on either side of Micah, life vests on. Even from a distance, he could see that they were vibrating with impatience, annoyed that they had to sit and stay.

He remembered feeling like that, needing to run and roll, to burn off all that excess energy. His parents hadn't allowed him the freedom to explore his world. His earliest memories were of his father telling him to stand up straight, arms at his sides, chin high. He had to keep his clothes and room spotless, his shoes shined, and his hair carefully combed. Spare time was to be spent studying or excelling at carefully chosen physical activity: swimming training or cross-country running, sports that would be the building blocks to his career in the armed forces. He hadn't been allowed to join the local football team, to play street cricket with the other kids. No, he was The General's son, and he'd never been allowed to *play*.

Thadie encouraged the twins to play, explore, to engage with the world. He was angry with her but she was an excellent mum, he couldn't have asked for better.

Angus jammed his hands into the pockets of his linen shorts, enjoying the cool breeze coming off the ocean. It lifted his hair and plastered his button-down shirt against his chest. He looked down at his feet, thinking that he hadn't worn shoes since he arrived at Petit Frère. Normally that would be a good indication of a great mini break…

Today he felt miserable. It was late morning, and he still hadn't seen Thadie. Late last night, unable to sleep, he'd passed by her room on the way to the kitchen to grab a late-night snack and he'd heard her crying. It had taken all his willpower not to open her door, pull her into his arms and wipe away her tears.

He couldn't help her with this, Angus reminded himself. She had to accept his presence in her life in her own way and in her own time. Her non-wedding, his sudden reappearance in her life, sex, and her realising that she needed to be more than just a stay-at-home mum were all life-changing events and her world had been flipped over and upside down.

So had his, but he had far more experience in learning to accept the things he couldn't change and in playing the cards he'd been dealt. In war, you had to adapt quickly or else you, and your men, got sent home in a coffin.

She needed time and space to wrap her head around her new realities and he was prepared to give them to her. What choice did he have, as they were going to be in each other's lives for…well, probably forever? They were bound together by the awesome creatures they'd made.

The twins waved energetically and Angus

waved back, his thoughts still far away. He and Thadie were also, currently, connected by their incredible chemistry—their lovemaking last night had been off-the-charts hot. He'd had many lovers but making love to Thadie was a night-and-day experience compared to his previous encounters. He always made sure that his lovers enjoyed their time with him, but, with Thadie, her pleasure was of paramount importance. She was all that mattered…

He also felt mentally and, scarily, emotionally connected to her. Maybe it was because they had kids together, maybe it was because they'd always had this insane attraction, but sex with Thadie was different: deeper, hotter, a weird combination of emotional and mental and phys-ical. They fell into a rhythm, as if they'd been making love for years, knowing exactly how to make each other yearn and burn.

Since meeting her again, he felt equally thrilled and terrified, energised and unnerved. She had the ability to knock his life, and his am-bitions, off keel and he couldn't allow her that much power. Angus hauled in a deep breath and forced himself to be sensible.

Think, Docherty.

He liked her, appreciated that she was a won-derful mum and thought she was insanely hot.

But they weren't going to be a perfect TV family when they left the island.

That wasn't going to happen…

His boys were incredible. He was grateful to have found them. They would be a huge part of his life going forward. But he had a job to do, a company to run. A company that allowed him to serve his country, to use the skills he'd worked so hard to acquire.

His covert ops aside, Docherty Security also needed more time and input than he was currently affording it. He was opening a branch in Lahore, and another in Chisinau, the capital city of Moldova. There were decisions to be made, management to hire, premises to secure. Sure, Heath could make most of the decisions, but it was his company, his legacy under construction. Why would he want anyone else to be part of its design? And if he didn't keep an eye on every detail, a crucial component could be missed. Too many mistakes and he could lose his clients and acquire a bad reputation.

It was his name on the letterhead. His company was a direct reflection of him so it couldn't be anything but exemplary. Anything less would be a failure and he never failed…

The twins complicated his working life exponentially. A week ago, he could take off at a moment's notice on a covert op, and no one would question his absence or lack of contact. Angus rubbed his hands up and down his face.

Serving his country by undertaking covert operations, doing his part to make the world a safer place, was what he was born to do—it was the legacy he'd been handed at his birth, the only thing he took from his father. But, unlike The General, he didn't need compliments or kudos. He was all about the deed, not the recognition.

If he died while on a mission, he had a cover story in place: an innocuous death in a car accident overseas. But if he wanted to build a relationship with his sons, how would he explain why he was out of communication for weeks at a time? He could bamboozle the kids—they were young enough still—but not Thadie.

He didn't like keeping secrets from her.

The boat slowed down and Angus heard footsteps on the pier, turning around to see Thadie walking towards him. She wore a white lace, off-the-shoulder crop top over a white bikini top, and her ankle-length cotton skirt split open to reveal her toned thigh with every step she took. She'd pulled her braids into two complicated plaits, and she looked fantastic. But when she drew closer, he saw her red eyes and tight mouth.

'Morning,' he said, resisting the urge to reach for her.

Thadie placed her hand on his bare forearm,

just below the rolled-up sleeve of his shirt. 'I should not have said what I did. I'm deeply sorry, Angus.'

He took her hand in his big one and squeezed. It took guts to apologise, and he appreciated her doing so.

He'd accused her of being dishonest last night, but he wasn't being open either. There was no way he could tell her the truth. *Hey, by the way, being the founder and CEO of an international security company is not all I do. Three or four times a year, me and my team...'*

Nope, he couldn't do that. Firstly, what he did was highly classified. Secondly, he didn't want to expose her to that clandestine world. She and the boys were sunshine and light, he didn't want to explain that he frequently walked through darkness.

And, not even a week after meeting her again, he was questioning what he did and how he did it. This was a classic example of her ability to upend his world.

'It's okay, Thadie,' he assured her, wanting to get back to normal, whatever that was. 'It's a new road and we're both bound to stumble.'

Thadie looked out to sea and Angus followed her gaze. The boat slowed down and then Jago cut the engine. Within seconds, they were all, including Jabu, looking over the side into the blue-green water. He wondered what had caught their attention.

'Are you enjoying the island?' Thadie asked him. 'I hope it measures up to all the other places you visit on vacation.'

He flinched at her very unexpected question and hoped she didn't notice. 'What vacations?' he casually asked.

'Micah said that you take lots of vacations. He sounded quite jealous, by the way. He wondered how you managed to run your company and make time to take so many holidays.'

He couldn't tell her that this was the first 'holiday' he'd taken in three years, the first time he'd had some downtime in forever. 'I work hard and play hard.' He shrugged.

Thadie tipped her head to the side. 'Funny, but I can't picture it.'

His eyebrows lifted. He was too well trained to let his heart rate increase, but he was conscious of it wanting to inch up. 'You can't see me taking a holiday?'

She shook her head. 'No. I picture you chained to your desk, buried in paper, juggling ten calls, emails and a video-call all at once.'

It was a fair assessment of his life as Docherty Security's CEO. 'I do, now and then, leave my office and get away.'

It wasn't a lie, he thought.

Thadie pulled him back to the present by clearing her throat. When he looked at her, he caught the excitement in her eyes. 'So, last night you asked me about my plan,' she stated, sounding hesitant.

Right, before their fight she'd been talking about how unfulfilled she felt. 'Yeah?'

'I couldn't sleep last night and, after I stopped feeling sorry for myself—' he liked her self-deprecating manner, her ability to gently mock herself '—I started *thinking*.

'According to an Internet site tracking this stuff, I have one of the biggest social media followings in the country, around four and a half million. That's a lot of people,' she said, sounding amazed. Angus wasn't on social media, but he knew enough to be impressed. Four million people paid attention to her posts, to what she had to say.

'I then went onto some of the local fashion designers I love, and checked how many followers they had...'

Angus folded his arms across his chest, enjoying her fire. 'Not as many as you, I bet.'

Her smile widened and he felt as if he'd inserted his finger into the surface of the sun. 'Some have as little as thirty thousand followers. The top designer only had one hundred and fifty thousand. I think there might be an opportunity for me to leverage my social media following...'

Now, this was smart. 'How?' Angus asked, keeping one eye on the approaching boat.

'I promote them to my four million followers, and they take me on as an intern, as well as help me to develop my own fashion line. Obviously, I couldn't compete with them.'

'They all do the same thing, don't they?'

'Actually, they don't,' Thadie explained. 'Some do wedding dresses, some do high fashion, some easy-to-wear clothes. None of them does what I want to do.'

'And that would be?'

She nodded at the incoming boat. 'Kids' fashion. African inspired but with worldwide appeal. Strong fabrics, great colours, generous cuts.' Thadie bit down on her bottom lip. 'I think I want to launch a children's fashion line, Angus.'

It was a fantastic idea, and he had no doubt she'd do an amazing job. He couldn't stop himself—he was so damn proud of her, and thrilled by the excitement he saw in her eyes—he dropped his mouth onto hers, torturing himself with a brief taste of her mouth. He wanted to lower her to the pier, strip her out of that lovely outfit and see the sunlight on her skin.

He'd never felt like this about anyone before. Correction: he'd never felt like this before. This was territory he'd never explored, a minefield he didn't have the skills to navigate.

'Oooh, gross! Why are you kissing my mum?' Gus shouted from the boat.

Angus winced before turning around to face the twins' disgusted expressions and Micah's and Jago's amusement.

He rubbed the back of his neck, embarrassed. 'Uh…'

Thadie's hand touched the centre of his back.

'Distract and evade, Angus. Watch and learn,' she quietly murmured, before stepping around him and placing her hands on her hips.

'What did you guys see as you were coming in? Did you see a big, fat dragon? Or a mermaid with a glittery blue tail?' she asked them, sounding fascinated.

Being three, the twins rapidly forgot she and Angus had locked lips.

'No, Mum!' Gus replied, rolling his eyes as Micah lifted him from the boat to the pier.

'It was a huge whale, maybe as big as a house,' Gus babbled as Thadie helped him with his life vest. 'And, *Mum*, we slept on the beach, and I made a fire and we watched flying stars.'

Angus stepped forward to help Finn. His younger son looked up at him and Angus felt the punch of surprise to see his eyes on Finn's face. Would he ever get used to that? He didn't know.

'Hi, Angus,' Finn quietly said, as calm as his brother was wild.

'Hey, bud. Did you have a fun time?' Angus asked, dropping to his haunches to unclip his vest.

'Yes,' he replied, before releasing an annoyed sigh. 'It was a whale *shark*, which is a fish. Gus didn't make the fire, Micah did, and the stars were shooting stars! Gus never gets it *right*.'

Angus swallowed his smile as Finn turned around to hug Thadie, who was also on the balls of her feet, gathering her boys close. She shut her eyes and Angus watched them, a hard knot of something—it couldn't possibly be emotion, he didn't do emotion!—in his throat.

His family...*his*.

Dammit.

He was so caught up in the pretty picture they made—a gorgeous woman, two astonishingly good-looking boys, a flat, clear blue sea and bright sunlight—that he didn't hear Micah's comment to Jago or see their wide smiles. 'Right, well, that answers *that* question.'

CHAPTER EIGHT

THADIE TOOK ONE last look at the twins's angelic-in-sleep faces and closed the door to their bedroom.

Her twins were having the best time and an amazing holiday and that made her remember her conversation earlier with Angus about the holidays he took. What was bugging her and why did she feel as if he hadn't responded authentically?

Thadie leaned against the wall next to their bedroom, needing a moment before she rejoined Angus on the deck. There was definitely something he wasn't telling her. If asked, she couldn't explain how she knew, she just *did*.

What was he holding back?

And why hadn't she challenged him? This was where she'd gone wrong with Clyde. She'd let things slide, brushed away or ignored her concerns, her gut feelings. Why was she backsliding, revisiting old, and bad, habits?

*Just hold on, Le Roux, think this through.
Angus isn't Clyde and the guy has only been
back in your life for a week.* She and Clyde had
been together for nearly a year, she'd planned
on marrying the guy! Angus had been in her
life for less than a week. Sure, he was Gus and
Finn's dad, and they were sleeping together, but
that didn't give her the right to probe.

But the urge to push, to know, wouldn't leave
her. Thadie walked through the villa and out
onto the deck. Angus sat on a wide lounger, and
two glasses, one half full, and a bottle of red
wine rested on the wooden table next to him.
She poured some wine into her glass and took
a fortifying sip before blurting out her question.

'What aren't you telling me?' Thadie asked as
she plopped down to sit next to him.

'Where on earth did that come from?' Angus
asked her, his hand coming up to hold the back
of her neck.

She gulped her wine and lifted her shoulders
to her ears. 'I can't get rid of this feeling that
there's something you're not telling me.'

Angus sat up straight and kissed her bare
shoulder. Even though tiny flames of lust flick-
ered over her skin, and she wanted nothing more
than to kiss him, Thadie realised that her statement had hit a nerve.

Angus ran his finger over her shoulder and

traced the line of her off-the-shoulder lace crop, along the cords holding the triangles of her bikini up. 'Why don't we stop thinking tonight, Thads, and just feel?'

She gripped his hand, stopping any further explorations. 'Angus, stop trying to deflect me.'

His expression hardened, just a fraction. 'Stop asking me questions I can't answer.'

'Can't or won't?'

His thumb skated along the ridge of her cheekbone. He sighed and dropped his hand, looking frustrated. 'I'm trying to work something out. Will you give me the space to do that?'

Work what out? 'Will it affect the boys?' she demanded.

'No, it's a work thing.'

Angus pushed his hand through his hair. 'Thadie, it's a beautiful night, the stars are heavy in the sky, the sea is loud, and the breeze is warm. And you are gorgeous. Talking is not what I most want to do.'

Thadie looked at him, caught between wanting to pry and, well, wanting him. The look on his face as he lifted his hand to touch her, as if she were made of indescribably rare and precious material, swayed her from the mental to the physical.

Angus's index finger gently traced the outline of her nipple and she sucked in her breath, looking down to watch his tanned hand against the white lace. So hot. The thought whispered through her as he pushed the lace away to touch her, skin on skin. Angus lifted her so that her nipple was in line with his mouth. He tongued her, pulling her into his mouth, nibbling her with his teeth. She ran her fingers through his thick hair, tracing the shell of his ear, and the strong cords of his neck.

'I want you so much, Thadie,' Angus told her, his voice growly with desire.

How could she say no? She wanted him as well, as much, possibly more.

He rested his forehead between her breasts, still holding her, and she felt his hot breath against her skin. She didn't know what the future held, how much Angus would feature in their lives, or how to navigate her suddenly complicated future, but she knew she wanted to make love to this big, hot, secretive man. To have him in her bed...

For as long as he would stay.

'Take me to my bedroom, and love all the thoughts out of me, Angus,' Thadie whispered, her fingers dancing across his lips, his jaw.

Angus simply nodded, stood up and, after scooping her up—a feat, given her height and curves, she'd never thought was possible—carried her inside. Seemingly not needing to look where he was going, he kissed her while he navigated a path through the house, avoiding furniture, sculptures and a Lego robot Gus had left in the middle of the passage. In her bedroom, Thadie held onto him as he lowered her to her enormous bed and released a contented murmur when he settled into the V-shape between her legs.

This was where he belonged…

Pushing that thought away—*too much, too soon!*—she helped Angus rid her of her lacy top and bikini bra, watching as he shed his shirt with a one-handed tug. His naked chest touched hers and she tongued his flat, masculine nipple. Yum…

Angus released an inaudible curse and pulled back to tug her skirt over her hips. His eyes moved down, taking in her breast before moving over her rounded stomach to her bikini bottoms.

'I didn't take the time to look at you last time,' he told her.

She wished he wouldn't. 'I breastfed the babies, so my boobs aren't as great as they once were, and I have stretch marks,' she explained, feeling self-conscious. Silly, but she wasn't always as confident as the world thought her to be.

'I don't care,' he bluntly told her, and she heard the sincerity in his tone. He stroked his fingers across her caesarean scar, and she visualised it in her mind, a thin slash above her pubic mound.

'I'm not ashamed of that scar. If I didn't have it, I wouldn't have my—the boys,' she told him.

Tears burned her eyes when he dropped his head and placed a series of gentle kisses from one side of the scar to the other. It was both sweet and erotic, lovely and heart-poundingly sexy.

She was on the point of begging him for more when Angus slowly peeled her bikini bottoms down her legs, before rising to shed his shorts. Scars and kids and the future forgotten, Thadie stared at him, and Angus stood there, allowing her to look. Wide, big shoulders, big, muscled arms, that broad chest. He had sexy abs, but she also adored those long hip muscles, his lean, powerful thighs, and his scar was proof of the battle for life.

Angus managed to combine his blunt good looks—he was the definition of masculinity— with the suggestion of speed. Silent, but obvious power. But under that fine package was a man who could make her feel, make her want, make her need. She enjoyed his body and was impressed by his quick, sharp mind but his effect on her emotions scared her. He could melt her mind...

But...*dammit*...she couldn't resist him. She always, as long as she breathed, would want him but she wouldn't let herself love him.

Angus leaned over her to place his hands on the cool cotton next to her head and dropped his mouth to cover hers, taking his time to explore. Last night, they'd rolled around the bed, their kisses desperate, their hands insatiable. But tonight was different. He seemed to want to take his time, to draw pleasure from the journey and not the destination. Thadie tried to touch him, but he moved his hips, nudging her hand away.

'I want to play,' he told her. 'I want to make this last, draw it out until we are both breathless with need.'

She didn't think that was a good idea. Hot and fast sex could be categorised as a biological need—they were just a pair of healthy adults enjoying themselves. But slow sex, sweet sex, profound sex was...

Making love.

She couldn't allow her feelings to get involved because she had work to do, on herself, for herself. She needed to find out who she was, and how she was going to navigate this world without reference to anyone else. But Angus had a way of making her dream in glorious technicolour. And feel far too much...

'Angus, please,' she begged, a couple of deep breaths away from releasing a sob. They had to treat this, them together, sex, as release they both needed.

She couldn't afford to allow an emotional connection to develop and deepen.

Finally, weeks, *years* later, Angus pushed inside her and Thadie wrapped her legs around his back, pulling him closer. As he pushed her higher and higher, the physicality of the act, her yearning for release, calmed her whirring thoughts and she simply shut down. All she cared about was the crashing release he could give her. Her hands flew over his thighs, back, up and down his butt, stopping occasionally to dig her fingernails into his skin. One of her braids dropped over her eye as she thrashed her head from side to side, hovering, hovering...

She floundered on the edge of that fireball of pleasure, holding herself back from stepping in, needing another few moments of anticipation.

'I can't hold on, Thads,' Angus muttered against her mouth. Placing his hand between their bodies, he found her and stroked with just enough pressure and intent. One minute she was on the outside, the next she was burning up, in the best way possible. She became the sun, and the stars, danced with the moon and skated along the Milky Way.

Angus, breathing heavily, rested his weight on one hand and gazed down at her. He pulled her braid off her face and tucked it behind her ear. Emotions, confusion mostly, jumped in and out of his eyes and she was relieved to know that he felt equally off-balance, as unsettled.

He didn't know how to handle the situation— any of it, including their crazy chemistry—either. And, strangely, that eased a great deal of her tension, calmed her washing-machine mind.

It was reassuring to know that he was also stumbling around in the dark.

While the island's staff transported their luggage for them to the boat to Felicite, and the private jet, Thadie walked down the beach with Angus, in sight but out of hearing of the twins.

Their holiday was at an end, and it was the start of a new chapter…no, the opening of a new book. Hopefully, the press attention about the wedding had died down and she could slide back into relative obscurity and life could go back to normal. Or, with Angus in their lives, a new normal.

Whatever that meant.

Thadie glanced up at him, his eyes shaded by expensive sunglasses. They'd been living in a bubble these past few days—him in her bed at night, making her sigh and making her scream—and they'd spent their days with the twins, swimming, snorkelling and making fifty thousand sandcastles on the beach. With good food, and unintrusive five-star service on a stunningly lovely island, their days, and nights, had passed in a happy, hazy dream.

But they were leaving this morning and reality lurked over the horizon, rough and tough and taking no prisoners. She and Angus needed to talk about his future relationship with the twins, but should they do that now, or on the plane, or should she wait until they landed back in Johannesburg?

'Did you hear back from any of your designers?' Angus asked her.

She'd sent them a 'would you consider this?' email and all but one had replied. 'Two turned me down, four are interested. All want to see my portfolio of designs before they commit to anything,' Thadie explained. 'And they want them quickly.'

'What's the rush?' Angus asked.

She shrugged. 'One of the designers is taking maternity leave and wants to get this sorted before she has the baby, another is in the process of launching an online store and a brick-and-motor boutique in London. I guess the other two want to see if I can work under pressure.'

'You'll get it done,' Angus assured her. While Thadie appreciated his support, she wasn't as confident. She wasn't sure she would be able to produce a portfolio of designs within a few weeks. Looking after Gus and Finn was a full-time job and she could see a lot of late nights in her future.

'What's your deadline?' Angus asked.

'Two weeks for one, a month for two, two months for the other one,' Thadie told him.

He winced. 'Two weeks? That's tight.'

He had no idea.

'My favourite designer is the one going on maternity leave. I like Clara, we've met a few times and I enjoy her. I think she likes me, and we could work well together. She's my first choice.' Thadie bit her bottom lip, frowning. 'But I don't think two weeks is feasible and I might have to give her a miss.'

'You need to try, Thadie, you'll regret it if you don't,' Angus told her.

She swallowed down a spurt of annoyance. Words like that were easy to say but when they got back to Johannesburg, she would resume her normal routine. It would be impossible to look after the boys and whip up a design portfolio. And it would take time to get them into a school.

By the time she got the kids into bed, she was exhausted, and her energy levels were depleted. She'd probably fall asleep at her desk. If she got as far as her desk.

Why hadn't she given this idea more thought

before reaching out to the designers? She should've waited until she got the boys into a nursery school and planned this properly. Instead of running headlong into the situation, not thinking it all the way through—just as she'd done with Clyde—she should've weighed up the pros and cons and made a more sensible decision.

But she'd remembered the approval in Angus's eyes, how impressed he'd been at her reaching out and chasing her dream and, basking in his approval—it had been a long time since she recalled someone being proud of her—she'd fired off those emails.

Such a reckless move…

Angus's arm landed on her shoulder, and his big hand cupped her arm and pulled her to his side. 'Relax, Thads, it'll be fine.'

She tried to smile, annoyed by his breezy attitude. He was so confident and had no idea how scary it was to attempt something new, putting herself out there, not sure if she could do what she'd breezily promised.

She wasn't a kid any more, a twenty-six-year-old with no responsibilities, someone who'd taken her time to get her degree. She was a Le Roux, had a dedicated social media following—a lot of them who were young mums who listened to what she said and watched what she did—and a press pack who'd dogged her every step because she was, because of her last name and ridiculously, South African royalty.

Thadie slapped her hand over her mouth, terror skittering through her. She stopped abruptly, her toes digging into the sand. 'What have I done, Angus?'

His hands skated up and down her arms. 'You're chasing your dreams, Thadie. There's nothing wrong with that.'

'You don't understand,' she gabbled, panic closing her throat as another thought hit her. 'If the press hears about this, I will be excoriated.'

'Why?' he asked, looking genuinely confused. 'You're going in a different direction. People do it all the time.'

'But if my designs aren't a success, then they'll say that I'm playing at fashion, foisting a sub-standard product on the public and thinking I can sell it because I am a Le Roux. If my designs are a success, then they'll say that it's only because I am trading on my name. That's if I get as far as launching a line. If they hear about me reaching out to designers and I don't follow through, or if none of the designers wants to work with me, then that's another story that'll dominate the headlines!'

Angus told her to take a breath and when she

did, he looked down at her, shaking his head. 'Don't you think you are overreacting a touch?'

Overreacting? Seriously? She started to blast him, then remembered that he didn't live in this country and that he'd only seen the video of her press conference because she was his client. Was she still his client? Did she still need a body-guard? She didn't know whether her and Clyde's bust-up was still dominating the headlines.

But that was, fractionally, off the point.

Angus had no idea that, as Theo and Liyana's daughter, she was often featured in society columns, and her engagement to Clyde, an ex-rugby player who was a national hero for being part of the World Cup winning squad, had set off a feeding frenzy. Her wedding woes had kept everyone entertained, there had been speculation about the health of their relationship and when she'd fired Alta as one of her bridesmaids that story had entertained the public for weeks.

Her non-wedding and viral video had been, as far as the press was concerned, an abundance of riches.

Angus, a Scot and someone who didn't overly concern himself with the shenanigans of A-List South African society, had no idea how news-worthy she was.

'I am not overreacting,' she said, through grit-ted teeth.

Angus linked the fingers of one hand with hers. His eyes, the same colour as the sun-speckled ocean behind him, connected with hers and she couldn't help herself, she tumbled into all that blue. 'I get that you are scared. Trying something new is always frightening. But this is your time, you need to grab this opportunity and do something for yourself.'

He didn't understand—it wasn't that easy. 'I have boys to raise. They take up a lot of time. I haven't sketched for four years. I have no idea if I even remember my training. I have wedding gifts to return—'

'You've given me lots of reasons why it won't work,' Angus agreed. 'Now give me a few reasons why it will work. Why doing this will be one of the best decisions you'll ever make.'

She had to think, and she couldn't do that when he was so close. Didn't he know that he short-circuited her brain? She walked away from him and scuffed the sand with her bare foot, scowling at the second, smaller speedboat the staff were loading. She looked at the twins, who were by the rock pool, looking into the shallow depths.

Thadie folded her arms across her chest, her heart thumping.

'Well?' Angus asked from behind her.

She wrinkled her nose, not happy that he

wouldn't let this go. 'I was good,' she reluctantly admitted. 'I was told I had talent.'

'Talent doesn't just disappear so, with a little practice, I'm sure it will all come straight back to you,' he told her. Thadie felt her bands of tension loosening, a little confidence returning.

'I'm smart. I mean, I'm not as good at business as you and my brothers but I'm not an idiot. I'll know if I'm being taken for a ride or being patronised. Or used.'

'That's a valuable skill,' Angus told her, sounding sincere. 'What else?'

She released a huffy sigh. 'Isn't that enough?' she demanded.

Angus simply widened his stance and linked his hands behind his back, looking thoroughly at ease. She knew he would stand there, like the soldier he'd once been, for as long as it took her to come up with an answer that satisfied him.

'I'm willing to learn, I *want* to learn. And I can work hard, Angus. I know that I look like a trust-fund baby, who has money at her fingertips but I know the value of hard work. My father had his faults, but he wasn't shy to put his shoulder to the wheel.'

He smiled at her, and an undefinable emotion crossed his face as he looked across the sand to see the twins climbing down from the rocks.

'Thads, that I already know.' He held out his hand, and she slid hers into his.

'Feeling better?' he asked, his tone gentle. 'A bit steadier?'

She was. It helped to talk through her fears, to have someone listen and respond, to give a masculine point of view. She wasn't brimming with confidence, but neither did she feel like a ripped-away leaf caught up in a tornado. She'd never had a conversation like this with Clyde. She hadn't been able to share her fears and doubts. It was wonderful to bounce ideas off him, and to feel supported. What would it be like to have him permanently around—?

No, don't think like that, Thadie. That way madness and disappointment lay. She couldn't start to rely on him and then, one day, look for him and he wasn't there. Just like her parents and Clyde.

'What if you stay here for another week, Thads?'

Thadie lifted her hands, confused. 'What? Why?'

'You said that the resort is empty for another five days, right?'

She nodded, not knowing where he was going with this.

'Stay here, draw, think, take a break. Re-charge all those batteries so that you can hit the ground running when you get back. Take some time for yourself…'

Uh, she was a mum, she had the twins to look after, as she told him. Angus shook his head, not convinced. 'The boys will be absolutely fine without you for another few days. It's five days, Thadie, not five months or five years. Jabu will keep them occupied during the day, Micah and Elle will look after them at night and I'm sure that Jago would pitch in as well. I would stick around if I could, but I need to get back to London.'

Angus placed his big hand on her shoulder, looking serious. 'I think you need to do this, I think you should take some time on your own. You deserve it.'

The thought was both entrancing and terrifying. 'But what would I do?' she wailed, shocked that she was considering his suggestion.

He shrugged. 'Get a massage, get lots of massages. Read, sleep, think. Sketch your designs—'

'I don't have paper or any art supplies,' Thadie told him, happy to poke a hole in his runaway-train plans.

'Make a list and I'll see that what you need comes back with the boat,' Angus told her, his eyes car-crash serious.

She bit her lip, excitement and terror mixing

in her stomach. 'I don't think… I don't know, Angus.'

'I do,' he told her, his thumb stroking her cheekbone. 'Trust me on this.'

'Angus!'

He turned round, smiling. He instinctively dropped to his haunches as the boys hurtled towards him, ready to be scooped up and spun around.

Angus carried their boys across the sand, tucking them under his arm like human rugby balls, and Thadie hung back, entranced as she watched her lover interact with their sons. There went her entire world, she admitted.

Two small boys and one very big man.

She knew she shouldn't be, that it was emotionally dangerous, but right now, for the next few moments, she'd allow herself to be completely, irretrievably drunk-on-emotion crazy about all three of them.

Trust him, he suggested. She was, she reluctantly admitted, starting to.

CHAPTER NINE

ANGUS HAD BEEN travelling for fourteen hours, crossing the Indian Ocean twice, but when he stepped onto the deck of Rock Villa and saw Thadie curled up on the lounger next to the infinity pool, a half-empty glass of wine on the table next to her book, he felt as if he was in the right place, at exactly the right time.

He'd sat on the Le Roux plane, talking to various members of Thadie's family, helping to keep the boys entertained, and with every mile that had passed, the rock in his stomach had got heavier. His gut had started screaming that this wasn't where he was supposed to be, what he was supposed to be doing. He needed, for a few more days at least, to be with her. He knew it wasn't a clever move, he should be putting distance between them, emotional as well as physical, but the compulsion to return to Petit Frère was, like his compulsion to fly to Johannesburg after seeing that video, too strong.

She was the moon, and he the tide. One of these days he was going to have to learn how to break their connection because he had a company to run, a legacy to create and he didn't have time for unscheduled disruptions to his schedule.

But that was next week's problem.

His footsteps made no noise as he crossed the deck to drop to his haunches next to her, using one finger to push a bright braid off her cheek. His heart stuttered, and he sighed as he looked at her wide, lovely mouth, the long eyelashes on her cheek. She wore a low-cut vest top without a bra, and her full breasts tempted him to touch and taste. Pulling his eyes away, he smiled at the strip of bare skin between her top and her silky sleeping shorts, printed with… He looked closer. Were those tiny, perfect sketches of positions from the Kama Sutra? He squinted and his eyebrows lifted… Right, that one needed incredible flexibility.

He smiled, entranced by the thought of seeing how many positions they could get through over the next few days. Quite a few, he reckoned.

And he'd get to that. Right now he just needed to breathe and be. He could stare at her forever, content to inhale her perfume, to trace his eyes over every luscious curve.

Her eyes fluttered open, and he smiled at her dazed look, and watched as her hand came up to touch him. 'So real,' she murmured. 'Wish you were here.'

Her eyes closed again, and she rolled over, pulling her long legs up and settling back into a deep sleep.

'Oh, no, you don't,' he said as he stood up, bent down and scooped her up and into his arms. 'I know that I said you should sleep and relax, and you will, but not for a little while yet.'

He carried her across the deck and into the house, enjoying her look of wide-eyed amazement. 'Angus?'

He dropped a kiss on her nose. 'Hi.'

'Uh…hi,' she said as he lowered her onto the mammoth double bed in the master bedroom. 'What are you doing here?'

He kissed the spot where her neck and jaw met and painted her jaw with tiny kisses. 'Right now, kissing you.'

She pushed at his shoulders. 'I don't understand. You were flying back to London!'

'I flew here instead.' He lifted his head to smile at her. Damn, he was ridiculously happy to be here, in this big bed with her, the sound of the sea hitting the shore, moonlight pouring in from the open doors. 'I thought you might be lonely.'

'It's only been a little more than half a day, Docherty,' Thadie dryly told him. That didn't, he noticed, stop her from yanking his shirt out of his trousers and trying to pull it up and over his back.

He pulled his shirt off, and reached for her vest top, bright white against her stunning, smooth brown skin. 'Well, I was lonely without you,' he told her, placing his mouth on hers. She seemed to melt a little into the bed, a little into him, and against her lips he felt her smile.

But he still needed, crazy but true, a little reassurance that she was happy he was here, that he wasn't intruding on her space. He might feel as if they'd known each other forever but it had only been a little over a week, ten days since he'd dropped back into her life.

'Is it okay that I came back?' he asked, pushing his hands inside her sleeping shorts and down her hips. Nearly naked, he thought, one of the many ways he liked her.

Thadie used her core muscles to sit up, and echoed his movements, pushing his shorts down his legs and wrapping her hand around his shaft. She ran her thumb across his tip, and everything faded, there was just him and her and the pleasure they could generate together. When she held him like this, he didn't care whether he was intruding, whether she needed time and space and quiet.

He needed her. Angus needed to feel her wrapped around him, his tongue in her mouth, her amazing legs around his hips, to hear her gasps and groans, her wet, hot heat around his length. She was the closest thing to a home he'd ever experienced.

'It's not okay that you took so long to come back,' Thadie said as he parted her legs and slid his hand over her feminine lips, testing her readiness for him. The sound she made was part sigh and part sob, and he positioned himself at her entrance, sliding his tip inside.

He intended to take it slow, to savour the moment, but Thadie had other ideas. She lifted her hips, he found himself inside her and he was lost.

And found.

Discombobulated and delighted. And very much not in control.

The island wasn't very big, and they walked it in an hour, following the wooden path that took them through the jungle-like foliage, across the huge granite rocks and over rock pools and coves. It was lovely to be alone on the island—when she'd heard she was going to be the only person on the island, Thadie had insisted that the staff take a vacation, she didn't need looking after—and even better that Angus was here with her.

She looked at his broad back as he walked the path in front of her, his board shorts riding low on his hips, the pre-dawn light accentuating the deep valleys of his spine. They'd got, maybe, a couple of hours' sleep last night, and had reached for each other time and time again, unable to get enough of each other. She was both exhausted and wired, and comprehensively thrilled to have more time alone with him.

And when Angus had suggested that they watch the sunrise from the other side of the island, she'd sleepily pulled on a pair of shorts and a vest and followed him out of the door.

Despite knowing she had a life to figure out, a career to reinvigorate, she was in deep danger of following him anywhere.

Angus stopped, looked up at a granite rock and nodded. 'The view from up there will be amazing.'

Thadie squinted at the root-covered rock and shook her head. She had the upper body strength of a noodle and there was no way she'd managed to scramble up the side, even if the roots would hold her weight.

'The sunrise will be best from there,' Angus told her, excitement in his eyes.

'The sunrise would be great from the beach. Or even better from the deck, with a cup of coffee in my hand,' Thadie told him.

Angus simply grinned at her, backed away and ran towards the rock. At the same time his foot hit the root closest to the ground, he leapt up and grabbed a root high above his head and swung his legs onto the top of the rock, where he crouched looking down at her.

How did he do that? One moment he was on the ground, the next he was twelve feet in the air. 'That was marginally impressive, Docherty,' she told him, tongue in her cheek.

He shrugged, as if scaling a monstrous rock were nothing. He looked around and grinned. 'The rock has a flat section and an amazing view. Get your pretty butt up here, Thads.'

'Uh...*how*?'

Angus told her to stand on the lower root and reached down to grip her wrist. With a quick, sharp tug, he had her up on the rock standing next to him. Unlike her, he wasn't out of breath and Thadie realised how much pent-up power he had access to. Impressive indeed.

Dammit, everything about him was.

They settled on the flatter section on the rock, and watched ribbons of light creep over the horizon, splashes of pinks and purples and reds, and push up into the scattered clouds hovering in the distance. The sea was still and silent and it seemed to Thadie that the island was holding its breath, waiting for the light show.

They sat there in comfortable silence, happy to watch nature preen, taking delight in her many colours. When the sun was an orange ball resting on the horizon, Thadie finally turned to look at Angus, her nose wrinkling when she caught him looking at her.

'The show is out there,' she told him, sounding flustered.

'I'd much rather watch you,' Angus told her, his deep voice sliding over her skin. He stretched out his legs and placed his flat palms on the cool rock, conscious of Thadie's long, bare leg next to his.

There was no place he'd rather be than here, right now.

Thadie bit down on her bottom lip, before twisting her lips. 'Were the boys okay when you said goodbye to them? Were they upset?'

Angus wasn't going to tell her that they'd had a little cry when they'd woken up on the plane—Finn in his arms, Gus in Micah's—when they'd realised that she wasn't there, but had soon been distracted by ice cream and Ellie showing them a funny animal video on her phone.

At the airport, he'd hugged them goodbye, for long enough to make them squirm. And for Thadie's family to send him speculative looks. They knew, he thought. The members of her family were smart, smart people, they could add two and two and get four. The boys had his eyes, looked like him…you didn't need an advanced degree in genetics to work it out.

But the twins' paternity wasn't something he was going to discuss with her family. Not without Thadie's permission and certainly not when she wasn't present.

'The boys are fine, Thads, kids are far more resilient than adults give them credit for. And when we get back to the villa you can video-call and check in.'

'It was really hard to let them go.'

He'd seen the pain in her eyes and knew how much she'd struggled with the idea of handing them over, even if it was to the people she trusted with her life. 'I know.'

'It's strange being without them. I keep thinking of something I should do, looking around for them.'

'That's understandable. But having some time alone will be good for you,' he stated, then winced when he realised what he'd said. 'Except I gatecrashed your alone time.'

She leaned into him, her shoulder pressing against his. 'I'm glad you're here. I really am.'

Relief rolled over him, warm and wonderful. 'Although this place is stunning, I do need to do some work while I am here, so you'll still have plenty of time to think about the future, make a start on sketching your designs, and figuring out how to tackle your new career.'

Angus felt the vibration on his wrist and looked down at his state-of-the-art watch, on which was displayed a brief text. It was from his government contact requesting a meeting. Requests for meetings usually meant that there was a mission on the horizon…

Strangely, his heart didn't kick up with excitement, as it normally did. He lived for these texts, and silently cheered when they came through. It meant a break from his desk, from the most predictable and sometimes mind-numbing monotony running a huge company entailed. Missions meant danger, excitement and the thrill of knowing that he made a difference.

But his flight south last week had changed his life in a myriad small, and big, ways. Unscheduled flights, the twins, unbelievably amazing sex, wonderful conversation. His old excitement to undertake missions had also evaporated.

Now all he could think was…*what if*? What if something went wrong? What if he never came back?

He couldn't do it. The risk was too great. There was only one decision he could make. When he got back to the villa, he'd jump on his computer and send his contact a message, telling her he was out.

He would redeploy his team to other positions within Docherty Security, but he was out of the covert mission game. He had to put the twins' needs first. They needed a father, and he was going to be there for them. He couldn't be the father he wanted to be if he kept disappearing.

But he'd have to tell Heath the reason for his newly acquired interest in South Africa and why his jet would frequently be heading south of the equator from now on. Heath wasn't only his right-hand man, he was also his closest friend, and he couldn't wait to show him photos of Gus and Finn.

But how would he explain his relationship with Thadie…? How did he even explain her to himself? It was too easy to say they were simply connected through the boys, and would be for the rest of their lives…

No, he wouldn't allow himself off the hook so easily. She was the woman he craved. He couldn't get enough of her. He wanted to protect her, obviously, and the thought of her being hurt made his blood freeze. He loved making love to her, but he also enjoyed talking to her and appreciating her smart and unique take on life and the world around her. She didn't bore him and he felt it would take many lifetimes for that to happen.

He couldn't imagine his life without her in

it. But neither could he make the mental leap to anything more solid, committed, permanent. He was becoming increasingly aware he couldn't stay away from her, but he was living in no man's land, unable to commit to her, ask her for more. And what did she want? She was also in a state of flux, needing time and space to plan her new life. For goodness' sake, she'd been about to marry someone else not even two weeks ago!

This was all happening too soon, too fast.

'What are you expecting from the next few days, Angus?' Thadie quietly asked, her eyes still on the one-hundred-and-eighty-degree view of the Indian Ocean in front of them. How did she manage to track his thoughts, home in on what he was thinking?

He thought about making a joke, saying something about good food and great sex, but swallowed that inane reaction. He honestly didn't know. When he'd left her, he hadn't thought further than getting back to her, seeing her huge smile, hearing her laugh and getting her naked. For a guy who planned everything to the max, who hated to fail, his flying to Seychelles to rejoin Thadie had been an impulsive, fly-by-the-seat-of-his-pants plan.

He liked her…

He liked her for many different reasons, but that didn't mean that he was falling for her, falling in—what an asinine expression—love. He'd outgrown the need for love in his teens. It wasn't something he wanted or needed, now or in the future. Of that he was sure.

But Thadie, as she always did—back in London, now—turned his world inside out, made him look at life differently. She had been, still was, the only person who'd ever managed to slide under his defences and tempt him to go beyond a sexual fling. Four years ago, he'd invited her into his flat, his life—telling himself he was safe because it was a temporary arrangement—and he'd rearranged his life to reconnect with her.

She made him yearn for more, for a life he'd never allowed himself to imagine.

She terrified him.

But he wasn't prepared for her to upend his life entirely. No man's land, that middle ground between nothing and emotional capitulation, was a safe place to hang out.

He lightly touched her back and waited for those amazing eyes to meet his. 'Our boys will have a mum and dad, and sometimes I'll be with you, them, and sometimes I won't. Thanks to video-calling, I can be on the other side of a screen in a heartbeat.'

'And you and me? What happens with us?' Thadie quietly asked. 'Where do you see this going?'

He thought for a moment, not knowing how to answer her. Eventually, he spoke, and his words were the best he could do. 'Does it need to be defined? We're modern, busy, independent people, and while I wish we both weren't so busy and could take the time to get used to everything, I'm grateful for the little time I can spend with you.'

But damn, he wanted more... He shouldn't but he did.

He forced himself to smile and when her lips started to curve, he bent his head to gently nip her shoulder. 'I can give you a plan for the next few days, that's the best I can do. I'll spend some time working, you'll spend some time thinking and sketching, and in between we'll try and get through all the positions on your sexy shorts.'

It took her a few seconds to make the connection, and her laughter rolled over him, deep and dirty. She gripped his jaw in her cool hand and dropped an open-mouth kiss on his lips. 'Deal! You're strong and I'm flexible, let's give it our all.'

She was flexible? Interesting, Angus thought as he followed Thadie to her feet. Trying out all those positions might put his back out, but he was game. What red-blooded man wouldn't be?

'What time will the helicopter get here?' Thadie asked Angus as she smacked the button of the coffee machine to dispense two espressos into tiny mugs. His ringing phone had woken them up shortly before six this morning and Angus had walked onto the deck to take the call.

He'd spent the next half-hour on the phone and when he'd returned, he'd told her that he had to leave, that a privately hired helicopter was on its way from Mahé to collect him and ferry him to Seychelles International Airport where his jet was parked.

He glanced at his watch, a vintage, rare Rolex. 'Ten minutes or so.' He sipped his coffee and ran a hand through his wet-from-his-shower hair. 'I'm sorry to leave after only two days, Thadie. I wanted more. But I have a crisis at work.'

'I'm sorry you have to leave too.' The past two days had been some of the best of her life. They hadn't done much work or, in her case, much thinking or sketching, but they'd talked a lot, laughed more and loved as hard and as often as they could.

Angus ignored the cup she held out to him, choosing instead to haul her against him, wrapping his big arms around her body. With him, she felt feminine and lovely, even petite. Protected.

She stood on her toes and pushed her nose into his neck, trying to imprint his hard body and clean, masculine, soap-and-sea scent onto her psyche. She didn't want him to go. He belonged here, with her.

She'd been avoiding the thought, pushing it away but...*damn*. She was crazy about him, a heartbeat away from falling in love with him. Again. And the solid gold truth was that they belonged with him...her and the two little guys they'd made on a cold night in London.

Terrifying but still true.

'I want to tell them about you,' she murmured, her words muffled.

He pulled back and Thadie lifted her eyes to meet his, the same blue-green colour as the ocean below them. She clocked his surprise, the burst of pleasure. 'You're ready to tell the twins about us?' he asked, sounding delighted.

Thadie nodded, smiling. 'And my family. Though, to be honest, I'm pretty sure they've worked it out already.'

He kissed the tip of her nose, her cheek, the side of her mouth. 'Thank you,' he said, squeezing her tight. 'I'd hoped but...when?'

Angus released his tight grip on her and Thadie took a deep breath, feeling her lungs expand again. 'We can do it when you come back to Johannesburg,' she suggested. 'When *are* you coming back?'

'I plan on being here the weekend before you pitch your designs.'

How was she going to cope with not seeing him? Missing him was going to become her favourite thing to do. 'It's going to be a nightmare,' she whispered.

'It's going to be tough with you trying to look after the boys and get your designs done.'

Ah, that wasn't what she'd been thinking about but that too.

'I'd like you to consider hiring an au pair,' Angus suggested.

Where did *that* come from? She looked at him, horrified. 'You know how I feel about nannies and au pairs, Angus. That's not going to happen.'

'Just hear me out, sweetheart. I get your antipathy towards the idea, but you are looking at it through the eyes of a little girl who never saw her parents. You associate au pairs with being neglected and being left alone. Am I right?'

Yes, okay. She shrugged.

'I'm not asking you to hand over the boys to an au pair, but what if an au pair came to the house and watched over the twins? You would be in your study working and you could be in shouting distance if anything happened. Obviously, the point of having her there would be to allow you to work, but if Gus and Finn wanted you, you're on the other side of a doorway. You're still *there*.'

It was tempting but it still felt like a cop-out. As if she was handing over her kids to a stranger.

'Thads, I am worried that you have too much to do and not enough time to do it,' Angus told her, and her head flew up at the concern she heard in his voice. 'I want you to start designing again because I know you love it and it's something that's yours, and something you do well. But you can't do everything alone. Within a week, after running after the twins and working at night, you'll be cross-eyed with exhaustion. You can't be creative, do your best work, when you can't function because you're burning the candle at both ends.'

'You work hard,' Thadie countered. She'd listened in on some of his work conversations these past two days, with his permission, and knew that he juggled a dozen balls at any one time.

'But I have people I delegate to. You don't and your job is a hundred times harder than mine. I'm not juggling two kids and trying to get a new career off the ground,' Angus explained.

She put her hand on her heart, blown away by his words. The fact that he was trying to make her life easier, his interest and support, told her that he didn't just see her as a mum, but as a woman, and that he believed in her talent and wanted to support her.

So this was what having someone in her corner felt like. She felt a little of his confidence seep into her, and her breath evened out. She wasn't alone, not any more.

If she looked at his suggestion unemotionally, hiring an au pair made sense. An au pair looking after the twins at home, where she could keep an eye on them, seemed the perfect solution. She was not her parents and making her life harder for herself was not going to change her childhood.

She bit her lip and nodded. 'Okay, yeah, I can look into hiring an au pair,' she told Angus.

His broad smile made him look years younger. 'Excellent! That's a really good answer, Thadie.'

She caught a strange note in his voice. 'What do you mean by that, Docherty?' she asked, frowning.

'Well, because you are interviewing three au pairs next week, the day after you get back. They are from the best agency in the city and have brilliant references.'

She'd walked right into that. 'We've got to talk about your tendency to take charge, Angus,' she muttered. 'What if I said no?'

'I was banking on you being sensible,' Angus told her on a slight grimace. He looked down, then back up to her, concern flickering in his eyes. 'You've got the right to do something for yourself, Thads, to chase your dreams. I just want to make it as easy as possible for you to do that.'

Thadie kept telling herself that she couldn't fall in love with him, or not fall any deeper in love with him than she already was, but how could she stop herself when he said things like that? It was impossible. He was a great-looking guy with a body he used to make her weep and scream with pleasure, but when he dropped his guard and got real, she wanted to shove her hand into her chest, snap off her heart and hand it to him.

She was pretty sure it was already in his possession.

Angus cocked his head and a couple of seconds later Thadie heard the whomp-whomp of an approaching helicopter.

'I'll see you the weekend before your big presentation. I'll fly in on Friday evening, and I'll keep the boys occupied Saturday and Sunday if you need to work.'

Knowing he'd be around that weekend to help out with the boys was such a relief because her brothers and their fiancées were attending a wedding in Cape Town and Jabu was unavailable.

'Thank you,' she told him, dragging her mouth across his. 'I'd give you more of those if I could.'

The pitch of the helicopter's engine changed, and Angus softly cursed. 'They are landing on the helipad. I've really got to go.' He didn't move away, and his eyes darkened with desire. 'Where?' He murmured the question, his voice a couple of octaves lower. 'Where would you kiss me?'

She touched the tip of her tongue to her top lip, feeling her nipples contract and lift the material of her T-shirt. 'Everywhere…' she boldly told him.

His phone started ringing and Angus closed his eyes, his expression irritated. 'You'd better go,' she told him. 'You're wanted.'

'No, *you're* wanted and there's not a damn thing I can do about it now,' he said, stepping away from her. 'I'll call you later.'

Thadie grabbed his arm to keep him from walking away and kissed him again, trying to delay the moment when he walked out on her. 'Thank you,' she told him, hoping he heard the gratitude in her voice and saw it in her eyes. 'For being supportive and for sorting the au pair… well, *everything*.'

He looked thoughtful. 'You can thank me with phone sex, later,' Angus told her with a naughty grin, kissed her again and strode out of the front door to Rock Villa.

Thadie wiggled her bottom and realised that she was quite looking forward to *that*.

CHAPTER TEN

HE FLEW INTO Johannesburg Saturday afternoon, delayed by a massive system dumping a ridiculous amount of snow on Gatwick's many runways and the breakdown of one of the snowploughs. And as they were waiting to be de-iced—which involved some special chemical that had to be sprayed over the jet—an emergency landing was called and they had to go to the back of the queue to be de-iced again. And then the airport was declared closed due to the snow and only opened six hours later.

His patience, by the time he made it from London to Johannesburg and then to Thadie's house, was running low. But seeing the boys hurtling out of the house to greet him with hugs before they ran back inside reminded him why he'd made the ridiculous ten-hour flight and battled Johannesburg traffic.

His boys. His woman. As always, his heart thumped with excitement, then seemed to stop, slam on the brakes. Was this how he was going to feel from now on, both elated and petrified? And if so, would he ever get used to it?

Thadie leaned against the doorframe to her house, dressed in a loose, off-the-shoulder cotton top and, low on her hips, battered denim shorts. A wide black band held her braids back from her head and he caught a glint of the diamond stud in her belly button. Angus felt a wave of lust so staggering that for a moment, he thought he might collapse on the ground.

Lust? Sure, it was there, it always was. But, more than that, he felt as if this was where he needed to be, a sense of being in the right time and place.

He'd felt something similar four years ago, but it had been a vague, nebulous, unidentifiable emotion. He had no doubt what it was now. He felt as if he'd come home.

Yeah, the boys were amazing, but wherever she was was where he was meant to be. Another scare-him-to-his-soul thought.

Thadie smiled at him, her eyebrows rising. 'Angus, you're here.'

'Finally,' he said, walking over to her. He held her face in both his hands, looked down at her and smiled before swiping his mouth across hers. She sighed, softened against him and returned his kiss, her arms wrapped around his back, pushing her lovely body into his. She needed, he realised, the connection as much as he did.

They kissed for long, lovely moments. He'd had a long two weeks and a frustrating twenty-four hours, and within Thadie's arms was where he needed to be. Until he felt a tug on his trousers and looked down at his oldest son, unimpressed by the amount of attention he was giving his mum.

'Angus, you need to come and see our Lego car!' Gus shouted, tugging some more. Angus rested his forehead against Thadie's and linked his fingers with hers.

'Sorry, I'm so late, I tried to get here sooner,' he told her.

'I'm just glad you got here at all,' Thadie told him. 'That storm was nasty.'

'Angus!' Finn shouted.

'Hold on, Finn,' he said, pulling back to look at Thadie. He'd expected red and tired eyes, for her to look stressed and harassed. But her eyes were clear, and he caught the pride and satisfaction in her eyes. 'You finished your portfolio, didn't you?'

She danced on the spot, her smile wide. 'I did! I couldn't sleep last night so I got up and worked.'

'I'm so proud of you, Thads.'

He pulled away to head back to the car to get

his laptop, suit and overnight bag. Knowing he was returning to sunshine and blue skies and hot days, he'd placed an online order for clothes and opted to have them delivered to Thadie's house where, she told him, they now sat in her walk-in closet. He couldn't wait to pull on his board shorts and hit the pool.

Unfortunately, the thing he most wanted, and that was to take Thadie to bed, would have to wait. Phone sex was great but wasn't a patch on the real thing.

'Why do you have a suit bag?' Thadie asked him when he pulled it off the back seat of his Range Rover. He knew he'd need wheels if he was going to be in and out of the city, so his car was another recent, and very convenient, pur-chase.

'I have a meeting on Monday morning in Sandton,' he told her.

She took the suit bag from him, pulled down the zip and released a low whistle. 'Armani, black. White shirt, red tie. Power suit,' she said.

He draped the strap to his laptop over his shoulder and picked up his small suitcase. 'I thought I could meet my potential client, you can meet your designer friend and I can take you to lunch afterwards, and we can celebrate your amazing new venture.'

'You're so sure I'll get this right,' she told him,

her free hand sliding into his as they walked back to the house.

That wasn't in any doubt. 'I know you will,' he told her. She was hugely talented, and she worked hard, why wouldn't she succeed?

She stopped and dropped a kiss on his bicep. 'Thanks, Angus. Thanks for believing in me.'

'Any time, sweetheart,' he replied, bending to kiss her head. He smiled down at her. 'As much as I like these gestures of affection, I'd far prefer for them to be X-rated. Can we put the kids to bed at, say, five?'

She laughed before wincing. 'Well, um, that's the other thing. Would you very much mind slipping into that suit and accompanying me to a charity fundraiser tonight?'

He'd rather pull off his toenails with pliers. 'Really, Thads? I just got in…'

She put her hand on his arm and looked up at him, her eyes beseeching. 'I know, I know… I'm sorry. I gave my apologies because I thought I would need to work but I've been feeling guilty about not going since I got the invitation.'

'Is it important to you?'

Thadie nodded. 'It's my favourite charity. They raise money to fulfil the dreams of kids who have a life-threatening condition. I thought I'd have to work so didn't think I could, but now I can. And it'll be really good publicity for the charity if my first public outing after the wedding—'

'Non-wedding,' Angus corrected. The thought that she'd come so close to marrying someone else irritated him.

'—is this function. And if I rock up looking absolutely fabulous, with an exceptionally good-looking man on my arm, well…'

He grinned. 'So, I'm just there as arm candy?'

'No, you're there because there's nobody else I'd like to take,' Thadie softly corrected him, her black eyes luminous. She wrinkled her nose in the way he loved. 'And because you're hot.'

He laughed at her, all the week's tension draining away. 'Sure, let's go to the ball, princess.' He gestured to the twins, who were sitting on the step leading into the house, their chins in their hands, looking impatient. 'Who will look after them?'

'Tumi, the au pair, is coming over at about six. They adore her. She'll feed them, bathe them and put them to bed. She'll also stay the night…'

His eyes narrowed, and deepened, at the sexy note in her voice.

'To reward you for putting on a suit and tie, and making nice with people you don't know, I booked the penthouse suite at the Edward Hotel. It has a hot tub and a very big double bed.'

All the blood drained from his head at the

thought of being utterly alone with her, falling asleep with her naked and waking up to morning sex and not to two little boys jumping on his chest.

He kissed her, feeling six hundred feet high. 'I knew hiring an au pair was a great idea,' he smugly told her.

She narrowed her eyes at him, mock scowling. 'Stop smirking, Docherty, it's not a good look for arm candy.'

Angus followed her into the house, laughing.

Angus stood at the bar and watched Thadie work the room, bestowing her stunning smile on everyone she met. He sipped his red wine as she crossed the room towards him, and his weren't the only eyes following her. If she intended to show the world, and her ex, that she was just fine, she'd certainly delivered that message. Her outfit, tight satin tangerine-orange trousers and a sleeveless fitted top in fabric just a shade lighter, was one only a superbly confident woman would have the guts to wear.

Her sky-high silver heels took her height to six feet or so, and she wore statement diamonds in her ears and on her fingers and held an expensive-looking clutch bag in her free hand. She looked…well, amazing. His tongue kept wanting to fall to the floor.

But, strangely, she didn't look any better than she had earlier, dressed in a simple top and cut-off denims, or the way she'd looked on Petit Frère, a sarong covering her bikini. She was naturally lovely, inside and out. And now he was thinking in cliches...a new low.

But the fundamental truth was that she'd, in very little time at all, become a very big part of his life. She'd given him his sons, but she'd also opened herself up to him, was sharing her thoughts and feelings, dream and fears. And he'd started doing the same.

In a few short weeks, she'd become his closest confidante, the person he wanted to talk to the most. She was the first person he thought about when he woke up, the person he fantasised about at night. Over the past two weeks, his thoughts had often gone to her. He'd wondered how her day was going, whether she was happy with her work, imagined her sketching furiously, playing football with the boys on the green lawn behind the house, climbing into her large bed with a book.

Through frequent video-calling, he'd had glimpses of her day-to-day life, her world, and it fascinated him. With a little compromise, some rearranging of his schedule—he'd have to do a lot more work remotely—he could make Johannesburg his base, and her loud and noisy house his home. He'd be able to kiss Thadie's neck when he found her at the kitchen island making supper or, if she was running late, make it himself. He could easily imagine late-night, naked swims in her pool, making love to her outside on the loungers while the boys slept upstairs.

It could work, it should work. He wanted to be there for his boys, as much as he could be, and that meant relocating. The General had been present in his life but in a bad way. He wanted to be there for his boys, in all the ways his father hadn't been. He'd already missed out on three years of their lives, and he didn't want to miss any more or be a part-time dad.

And, while he was genuinely delighted Thadie had rediscovered her love of designing, thrilled that she was doing something for herself, he knew she still wanted a proper family.

Just a year ago she'd been prepared to marry someone she didn't love to provide a father for the boys. They had a much stronger connection than she and Strathern had, so Angus had no doubts about her agreeing to his moving in with her. They didn't need to get married or make huge declarations of commitment, not yet anyway. If whatever they had needed to be defined, they could do that later. They'd only reconnected a month ago, they didn't need to make promises or hard-to-take-back statements yet.

Yeah, he was edging closer to the boundary that separated No Man's Land from Commitment, but he could ease his way over. There was no need to rush.

It could work, he thought. It would work. 'What are you smiling about, my sexy Scot?' Thadie asked as she approached him.

Thanks to her heels, her eyes were nearly in line with his. 'Just that you look utterly amazing tonight, sweetheart.'

Her hand drifted over her hip. 'It's not exactly a my-heart-is-broken outfit, is it?'

He dragged his thumb across her exposed collarbone and watched as goosebumps appeared on her skin. He loved the fact that she was so responsive to him. 'We need to talk, Thads.'

She nodded. 'I know, Angus, and we need to tell the boys that you are their dad, but can we take tonight? I want us to have a night to ourselves before we talk about the boys and how we're going to co-parent and raise them when we're living a continent apart.'

He had a couple of ideas on how to get around that…

But her eyes, intensely dark, holding a million secrets and promises, begged him to push reality aside and live in the moment. He was happy to stand here and make small talk as she charmed the room, knowing that she'd be his later, naked and glorious in his arms. He would be the one who'd be settling between her legs later, sliding inside her, making her his. Listening to her crying, or sobbing, his name as he pushed her to explore the range and depth of her pleasure. And when he was done, he'd start again…

When she woke up in the morning, they'd have sleepy, morning sex and, if he was lucky, more fun in the shower later. But all that would be overshadowed if he started a serious conversation tonight.

He brushed his lips against hers, in a brief, intense, promise-filled kiss. 'Sure, we'll talk later.'

She pushed her hand inside his suit jacket, and lightly drifted her fingers down his sides, and over his ribs. Silver sparks of desire glinted in her eyes. 'As soon as the speeches are done, we're out of here,' she promised him.

He closed his eyes, took a large gulp of his wine and he instructed his body to stand down, to wait. He'd been taught self-control and patience in the army, but one touch from Thadie could decimate that hard-fought-for trait.

Late Monday morning Thadie noticed Angus's car parked under her oak tree next to her garage and smiled, happy he'd made it home before her. Instead of going to lunch at a restaurant, they'd agreed to meet back here to talk. And maybe, because they had an empty house—the au pair had taken the twins to visit Jabu and then they had mini-football—they could indulge in some sexy times before Angus had to leave for the airport and she to await the boys' return.

Thadie pulled into her garage, switched off her engine and banged her hands against her steering wheel, excitement pouring off her in waves. Clara, her designer friend, adored her designs and they'd spent the morning making plans, bouncing ideas off each other, laughing and enjoying each other.

Over the next few weeks, they'd draw up legal agreements formalising their new venture. Thadie freely admitted that she was a bit rusty, she'd forgotten some of the finer details about garment construction, but there was nothing she couldn't relearn. What was most exciting was that she and Clara clicked, instantly and profoundly. Clara loved her presence on social media and they both believed in sustainable fashion and reducing the industry's huge climate-change footprint. They both loved nature, enjoyed the same colour palettes and Clara briefly picked Thadie's brain on childbirth and raising boys, as she was expecting a little boy shortly.

They were, as the Italians said, *simpatico* and Thadie could see them not only having a wonderful business association but building a close friendship. She was thoroughly over-excited. She couldn't wait to see Angus and tell him about her morning.

Under her excitement was a small stream of irritation because life and the universe had conspired to keep them from telling the boys Angus was their dad. When they'd returned to the house yesterday, Jabu had rocked up unexpectedly and whisked them away to visit the zoo, which had turned out to be a whole-day excursion. She and Angus had spent a quiet day, alternating between dozing, swimming, and making love. The boys had returned tired and crotchety and had been too exhausted for life-changing announcements. Thadie and Angus had reluctantly agreed to delay the news until his return trip.

In the meantime, she needed to find out what it entailed to add Angus as the father on the boys' birth certificates, to tag his surname onto theirs. She and Angus wanted joint custody, but did that need to be formalised? She needed to talk to her lawyer about that. And although Angus was paying for the au pair and would pay their school fees going forward, he wanted to put them on his medical plan and pay her maintenance, a ridiculously large figure she didn't need.

They had so much to discuss, and this was a

perfect time. They wouldn't be interrupted by their little men demanding attention.

Thadie left her car, slung her bag over her shoulder and walked up the path to her front door. She went inside, tossed her bag onto the coat stand and stepped out of her high heels. 'Honey, I'm home,' she trilled, shrugging out of her white linen jacket.

Angus walked through the half-open door from the entertainment deck, his sleeves rolled up and his tie pulled loose. He took one look at her face and grinned. 'You nailed it, didn't you?'

Thadie ran to him and he caught her, boosting her up so that she could wrap her legs around her hips. She kissed his mouth before pulling back, her smile ferociously wide. 'I *so* nailed it!' she crowed.

'I'm so proud of you, sweetheart,' he told her and she heard the pride in his voice. He walked her over to the kitchen area, placed her on the island and handed her an icy crystal flute, filled with pale gold champagne. 'Here's to your new venture, Thads.'

She looked at the glass, then at the bottle of champagne, one of the most expensive in the world, available only online and at specialist liquor stores. Organising the champagne would've taken quite a bit of work and she was touched.

'You didn't know that I was going to get this right, Angus.'

He touched his glass to hers. 'Of course I did,' he told her, standing between her legs. 'Now tell me all about it.'

She rattled on for twenty minutes, her mind jumping around, and she was sure she made little sense, but Angus listened patiently. Eventually, realising she was repeating herself, she sighed and shrugged. 'Sorry, I'm just fizzy with excitement.' And because she felt so alive, and because he was looking at her as if she'd hung the moon and stars—so powerful and special and clever—she threw her arms around his neck, kissed his jaw and placed her lips by his ear. They could talk later. 'Take me to bed, Angus.'

He glanced at his watch, groaned and pulled back so that she had to drop her hands from his neck. 'I'd love to, Thads, but we have just under an hour before I need to leave for the airport—'

'Perfect, we can spend it in bed.' Thadie shifted her butt to the edge of the island so that she could jump down but Angus's hands on her knees stopped her progress.

'We need to talk, Thadie. We keep getting interrupted or distracted, and this isn't a conversation I want to have over video-calling.'

She pulled a face. 'I'll talk to the lawyers about giving you joint custody, and yes, we'll add your name to their birth certificates. We'll have a meet-your-daddy party the next time you fly in and tell the boys that way. I'll take a tenth of the money you are offering me as maintenance, I do not need the monthly equivalent of a small country's gross national product. Have I forgotten anything? No? Well, then, let's go to bed.'

His hands tightened on her knees, his fingers pushing the material of her white linen trousers into her skin. 'I want us to move in together, to live together as a family,' he stated.

Maybe it was the champagne, maybe she was overloaded with excitement, but he couldn't possibly be suggesting such a massive change in their living arrangements in such an off-hand tone of voice. 'I'm sorry...*what*?'

He stepped back and rubbed the back of his neck with one hand. 'I want us to be a family, living together, raising our kids together.'

A thousand yeses, at full volume, built up in a tidal wave behind her teeth but she held them back, telling herself to calm down.

'But how would that work?' she asked, tightening her hands around the edge of the countertop and holding on as her vision tunnelled in and out. Why was she hesitating? He was offering her what she most wanted, him in her life, for her boys to have a father.

'I've thought this through. I'd essentially work from here. I'd still have to travel but Johannesburg would be my home base.' He looked around. 'I would move in here, initially, but we could find, or build, another house if we found we outgrew this one.'

'Why would we outgrow it?' she asked, confused.

He shrugged. 'Well, if we have more kids, we might need more space. And I'd need a home office—'

More children? What? How? Well, the how she knew, but why? And where was this coming from? And why did a small, low but insistent voice keep repeating, somewhere deep inside her, that something was wrong with his offer and that she needed to read the fine print?

Examine, *dissect*, the fine print.

'I'm sorry to sound stupid,' Thadie said, wincing at her ultra-polite tone, 'but I'm trying to get this straight in my head. We've known each other barely a month and you want to move continents and rearrange your business life to move in with me and the boys. *Why?*'

He looked at her as if he couldn't believe that she couldn't figure it out. 'I want to be a full-time dad. I don't want to see my kids via a video link. I want to see them every day. I want it to be the norm that I am here, the exception that I am away. I want to be *present.*'

Angus spoke before she could. 'My dad wasn't a dad, Thadie, he was my commanding officer from the day I understood what that meant. I mean to be a better parent, most definitely a different father. I want them to grow up knowing I would move mountains for them, but also knowing they can be, and do, anything they choose. And I want to raise them with you, because you are the antithesis of my cold, subservient, anal, unaffectionate mother.'

A frigid wave broke over her and shocked her back to reality. Right, it all made sense now. She had no problem believing Angus wanted to be a full-time dad; he was crazy about the boys and she could see him doing a fantastic job. She didn't have a problem with what he was saying, it was what he'd left out that was problematic.

Where did she fit in? How did he feel about her? His proposal sounded sane and sensible and clever and controlled but that wasn't what she wanted. She wanted wild and impetuous, and emotional and exciting. She wanted him to move in because of them, not because it was the most sensible option. Where was her 'I love you madly' or 'I can't live without you, and I don't want to'?

'I can see that you've given this a lot of

thought. Anything else?' she asked, her voice tightening with every word. She saw the look he sent her way and knew that he'd picked up on her tension.

He slid his hands into his pockets, his big shoulders lifting in a shrug. 'We like each other, we have an amazing time in bed, we enjoy each other's company. It makes sense.'

Did it? She didn't think so. With Clyde, she'd been prepared to give up what she wanted—a husband who loved her—to give her boys what they needed—a father. But she'd never do that again. She deserved more. And if she was going to take the risk of being hurt and disappointed, take a chance on love, then she wanted her partner to be facing the same risks, prepared to put his heart on the line too.

Angus didn't want to do that. He wanted the family, but he wanted to keep her at an emotional distance. Not happening. Not again.

She deserved love, a commitment. She was more than just a mum, and she was allowed to put herself first. She wanted it all, to be a great mum, to love and be loved, to have a career. And she wasn't prepared to settle for less.

And if Angus wanted to live his life with her, then he was either all in or all out.

She swallowed, and put her hand to her throat, feeling as if it was closing.

'Do you not think it's a bit soon for such a major move?' she quietly asked him, dropping to the floor. 'Don't you think we need more between us than like and some hot sex?'

'You were prepared to marry Strathern for less,' Angus stated. 'We have more going for us than you and he did, so I don't understand why you are hesitating.

'This is the right move,' he insisted. 'The four of us, together, is what is right for all of us.'

It might be right for *three* of them...

It wasn't right for her, not like this.

'You could do everything you suggested, move here, be a part of the boys' lives, but you could buy your own house and live there,' she said, twisting her fingers together, finding it hard to believe she wasn't throwing herself into his arms and kissing his face.

Angus looked as if he couldn't believe it either and he was starting to realise that she wasn't blown away by his suggestion. Thadie caught the confusion in his eyes, tinged with a hint of what-the-hell?

'Are you saying that you don't want me to move in?' Angus demanded, confusion deepening his Scottish accent.

'I'd love you to move in, Angus—'

'Then why are we dancing around this? Why aren't we using the precious moments before I have to leave to work out the future instead of having this crazy conversation that I don't completely understand?'

She bit her lip, wishing he'd wise up.

Angus threw his hands up in the air. 'Do you or do you not want me to move in, Thadie?' he asked, making an obvious effort to keep his tone reasonable.

'I do, but not because of the reasons you stated.'

He pushed both his hands into his hair and tugged. 'I thought you *wanted* a two-parent family, a father for your boys. You were prepared to marry someone you didn't love to give them that but when I offer it to you, you are baulking.'

Yes, she was. 'I am.'

'Why?'

Okay, it was time to put her heart on the line. 'Because I didn't love Clyde, Angus. He couldn't hurt or disappoint me. He didn't touch my emotions. You…well, you touch all of them.'

'I…*what*?'

She released a laugh that held no amusement. 'I am so in love with you, Angus. I tried not to be, but I didn't succeed. And I thought I could do the part-time relationship with you, having you drop into my life, turn it upside down and then leave. But I've been fooling myself. I don't think I can. I think I'd eventually begin to resent that you couldn't spend more time with me, be with me more.'

'I'm offering to do that!'

'But you are not offering me commitment, Angus. Or love.'

'It's too early to talk love, even if I understood what it means! But I do understand friendship, sexual heat, liking each other.' He shrugged, looking bewildered. 'But if you need me to marry you, I suppose I'll have to.'

Her heart cracked, splintered in two and dropped to her toes, as heavy as a steel ingot.

'I don't want you to offer to marry me because you think it's what *I* want, Angus.'

She took two paces, stopped, and took two more, needing to work out some of the energy building up inside her. 'I've realised that I don't need to marry anyone, that I can do life on my own, if I have to,' she explained.

'I am a complete person with or without a man. I'd only marry or live with a man if I knew, with every fibre of my being, that the man in question adored me, was head-over-heels, crazy in love with me, someone who couldn't live his life without me.'

She waited for him to say something, any-thing, but he just stared at her, his eyes more blue than green, dejected and annoyed. He hated this emotional stuff, hated that it wasn't regimented, that there weren't rules and regs that defined it. To him it was simple, they enjoyed each other in and out of bed, and they wanted the best for their sons, which was a two-parent, present family.

But living with a man who didn't love her would make her miserable. And, even if they could go back to simply sleeping together again, she knew this conversation had changed the dynamic between them.

She wanted more, he couldn't give it...

Yes, she was hurt, gutted, but at least he'd disappointed her early, and she hadn't had the earth beneath her entirely washed away. She'd be okay...no, that was a stretch. She'd find a way to function.

She was a mum, she had no choice.

It took all her guts, but she said the words, words that would hurt her but would, ultimately, protect their friendship and the boys.

'We need to call it, Angus, to stop sleeping together, to find another way forward,' she said. 'Our boys should be our highest priority, our only priority.'

'I don't understand this, any of this,' Angus muttered, his voice growly with banked-down emotion. 'I have done everything possible to show you that I care about you. I've criss-crossed goddamn continents for you. I gave up something I loved for you! Are you saying no?'

Gave up something he loved? What did he mean by that? She could ask for an explanation, and then they'd argue some more. They could go back and forth, slicing at each other with words as sharp as rapiers, but nothing would change the fact that she loved, and he didn't.

'This has been the most surreal conversation of my life and I don't know what else to say,' Angus said, his voice vibrating with an emotion she couldn't identify. She'd hurt him, and she knew he was wondering how and why his carefully planned day had gone so awry.

'There's nothing to say,' she told him, trying to smile. She took his big hand, holding it in both of hers. 'I still intend to tell the boys that you are their father, and you can stay here, in my spare room, until you find a permanent South African base. They need you in their lives, they *do*.'

'But you don't.'

Had he not heard anything she'd said? 'Of course, I do, but I need more than you can give,' she said, her voice sad. She stood up on her toes and kissed his cheek. 'You need to get going or you're going to miss your take-off slot.'

'That's it?' Angus asked.

Thadie nodded her head. 'Take care, Angus.'

And with her eyes brimming with hot tears, she walked out of the room.

CHAPTER ELEVEN

'MUM, ANGUS WANTS to talk to you,' Gus shouted. Thadie placed a hand on his small shoulder and looked down into the screen, wondering if the butterflies in her stomach would ever go away whenever she heard his name. Angus was sitting in a wide leather seat and, judging by the inky darkness she could see in the jet's window behind him, he was in another time zone. She took in his tight lips and stiff neck, and tried to smile but couldn't. It had been two weeks since he'd walked out of her life but his frequent calls to the twins hadn't stopped. He was as much a part of their lives as before, maybe even more so.

Thadie noticed the dark smudges under his eyes and his messy hair. He'd had another long day.

Finn came rushing up to them and held his hand out for the tablet. Thadie rolled her eyes as she handed it over. Her younger son had already spent ten minutes telling Angus about his day, in excruciating detail. What more could he have to say?

Angus spoke before he could. 'Bud, I need to talk to your mum so can this wait until we chat later?' he asked.

So he was still going to call the boys later? 'I want to know why—'

'Finn, *bud*,' Angus interrupted him, keeping his voice gentle, 'I want to talk to you but unless you're feeling sick or sad, it's going to have to wait until later, okay?'

Finn considered his words and nodded. ''Kay, bye!'

Finn shoved the tablet into Thadie's hands and ran to join his brother in the playroom. In the confines of her too-small screen, Thadie watched Angus take a slug of what looked like whiskey from a crystal tumbler, before resting the glass on his forehead.

When he looked into the camera again, he managed a rueful look. 'Just to tell you how my day is going, that conversation with my three-year-old was the most rational I've had today.'

She winced as she sat down on the wooden blanket box that she used as a coffee table. She missed him, yearned for him. She wanted his strong arms around her, for him to wake up beside her, to exchange long, lazy kisses, kisses with no beginning or no end.

She wished he loved her…

Oh, he probably did, as much as he could. But it wasn't enough.

Thadie started to ask him about his day, wanting him to tell her what had gone wrong, and then remembered that she couldn't open that door to emotional intimacy. Not when he'd made it very clear he wasn't prepared to walk through it.

'Are you okay?' he asked her.

No, she was thoroughly miserable, she felt as if she were walking around without a heart. But that was her fault—she'd handed hers to him, and he hadn't asked for it. 'I'm fine,' Thadie replied, internally wincing at her terse reply.

His eyes changed colour, turning cooler. 'I wanted to tell you that my lawyer received all the documentation regarding the boys. Thank you for allowing joint custody, for being so reasonable.'

That wasn't how she'd currently describe herself. Heartbroken, sad, joyless…they all applied. Reasonable? Not so much.

'You're a good father, Angus, I was happy to do it,' Thadie said, forcing the words out. They weren't the words she most wanted to say…

She was feeling tired and emotional, and it took all her effort not to let her always-close-to-the-surface tears roll down her face. She wanted to tell him she missed him. She wanted to ask him why he couldn't love her, why he, like her parents, couldn't give her what she most wanted. A soft place to fall, strong arms willing to catch her, a forever love to buoy and bolster her.

No, this wasn't on her and she needed to remember that. She'd done a lot of thinking and had had more than a few major revelations. Her parents were emotionally stunted and wouldn't have recognised love if it slapped them in the face. And she wasn't responsible for Angus's thoughts and decisions. She couldn't force him to love her, and she didn't want a love that was coerced. Love under those conditions would wither and die.

Thadie dug deep, sucked up another little bit of strength and forced what she knew was a brittle smile onto her face. 'Sign what you need to sign, and the lawyers can take care of the formalities,' Thadie told him. 'We'll tell them you are their dad when next you are in town.'

'Okay.' He pushed his fingers up and under his black-framed glasses—so hot!—to push his thumbs into his eyes. 'How is your new partnership shaping up?' he asked, his eyes still closed.

No, she couldn't talk to him, not yet. Not as they used to. It hurt too much. She looked away, pretending she'd heard a commotion. 'Hey, the boys are fighting, I've got to go.'

Without giving him a chance to argue, she cut the connection, and his face faded away in an instant.

It would help a lot if her love for him would die as easily and quickly.

A couple of days later, Angus stood at his office window, watching the bustling activity on the green, grey Thames in the distance. His office afforded spectacular views of the area, but he couldn't take it in. All he could think about was Thadie's pale and drawn face, the misery in her eyes.

Sadness he'd put there, all because he couldn't tell her what she most needed to hear.

What he felt. What he'd probably always felt, from the moment he'd met her in London.

The thing about love was that it was uncontrollable, that it wasn't something he could, through sheer hard work and determination, succeed at. There were too many variables, too much that could go wrong. He knew how to be a soldier, how to run a company, and he was learning how to be a dad. How to hand his heart over, how to love? He'd never been taught or been shown that.

If he tried to love her and failed—because how could he succeed at something he'd no training for?—he'd disappoint her further.

He didn't want to hurt her...

Correction, he didn't want to hurt her more than he was already doing.

He was doing the right thing, Angus reassured himself, rubbing his chest, somewhere above his sluggish, aching heart. He was hurting them now to save them both some big hurt down the line. It was a small skirmish to avoid a major, bloody battle later.

The aching pain and awkwardness would fade, and his craving for her would, oh, in seventy or so years, dissipate. At some point, somewhere down the line, they'd be friends again.

He missed her with every bloody breath he took.

Angus heard the sound of an incoming Skype call and glanced at his watch. His US-based chief of operations was calling in ten minutes early but that was okay, anything was better than standing here, feeling as if misery were eating him alive.

He picked up a remote control, pushed a button and his computer screen projected onto the state-of-the-art screen on the wall opposite. He blinked and rubbed his hands across his eyes but instead of his dark-skinned, burly Ving Rhames lookalike VP, he saw his youngest son on the wall.

'Finn, hi,' he said, confused. He'd spoken to the twins earlier, shortly after they woke up. He normally called them after their supper. Where was Thadie, and why did Finn have her phone? And how on earth did his three-year-old know how to video-call him?

Then he remembered his youngest's big brain: he asked complex questions and Thadie suspected he could already recognise basic words when she read to them. He could do basic addition and subtraction. Finn was super-smart, and it didn't take a genius to work out how to make a phone call.

'Where's Mum and Gus, Finn?' Angus asked, resting his butt on the corner of the desk.

Finn moved the phone and Angus saw Gus sitting at the kitchen table next to his brother. His oldest looked uncharacteristically sombre. Something was up with his boys, and he was in London, a continent away. Angus pulled in a deep breath, pushing down the panic that had instantly hit him. 'Hey, bud.'

Gus's eyes filled with tears. 'We miss you,' he said.

Angus felt as though he'd been hit in the gut. 'Me too, bud. Where is your mother?'

'She's in her office, Angus,' Finn answered him, turning the camera back to him. 'She's drawing but she keeps ripping the pages off and throwing the paper balls at the wall,' Finn told him, sounding bewildered. 'And she keeps saying a lot of bad words. She looks mad but we didn't do anything, I swear.'

'And she's crying,' Gus added.

'She's always crying,' Finn corrected him.

Angus pinched the bridge of his nose, feeling as if he'd been sucker-punched. Before he could think of what to say, how to console them, he heard a stream of Zulu. He looked at the screen and saw the chagrined expression of the twins' au pair.

'Sorry, Mr Docherty, I swear I only left them to go to the bathroom. Thadie left her phone on the dining table, but I didn't think they knew how to make video-calls.'

'It's not hard,' Finn told her, sounding a little belligerent.

Angus told the boys he'd speak to them later and sent them to their playroom. When Tumi confirmed they were out of sight, and hearing, he spoke again. 'They seem a little flat. Are they okay?' he asked.

She sent an uncomfortable look towards Thadie's study. 'Maybe you should speak to Thadie, Mr Docherty.'

'Call me Angus, please,' he told her. 'Look, I appreciate your loyalty, but their well-being is all I care about. Please, talk to me.'

She hesitated before speaking. 'All I will say is that Thadie and the boys are very close, and they pick up on her emotions. They've been quieter, clingier, less loud and energetic lately.'

Angus said goodbye to Tumi and instructed his PA to cancel his call with his VP. He locked his office door and sat down on his couch, his forearms on his knees. His world felt bleak and colourless, and he couldn't go on like this. Thadie was miserable and that was unacceptable. That, in itself, was a failure.

And all his fault.

Thadie was the strongest woman and he admired and respected everything about her. She hadn't let her parents' neglect harden or break her. And when she'd found out she was pregnant with his sons, she'd given up her dreams and career to focus her attention on them. She loved them so much that she'd been prepared to marry another man to give them a father.

All she'd wanted was for someone to put her first, to love her. To be the centre of someone's world.

Despite everything she'd been through lately, she'd still had the guts to tell him she loved him, the self-knowledge, respect and awareness to know what he was offering wasn't good enough. And it hadn't been. She deserved everything he could give her. To be the centre of *his* world.

But could he love her the way she needed him to? Was there even a wrong way to love? Was love something that he could fail at? Maybe, just maybe, he failed when he *didn't* love, not when he did.

Thadie deserved him to find his courage—emotional courage was on a whole new level—and commit to her, to love her with everything he had. Proving to his father that he was worthy of being a Docherty didn't matter any more. He was over that. He'd always thought that his company would be the legacy he left behind, but raising good men, men with integrity and loyalty, would be a far bigger gift to the world.

Being with Thadie, loving her, and putting a ring on her finger, would be the gift he gave himself. And if he didn't step up, he'd lose her. And not being with her, living his life loving her, would be the ultimate failure.

And the only one that would ever matter.

The next morning, Thadie walked into her kitchen, and headed straight to her coffee machine, reaching for a coffee mug. It was early, and she'd spent another night tossing and turning, missing Angus with every breath she took. She shoved her cup under the spout and hit the button with the side of her fist.

When would her broken heart start to heal? Would it? She hoped so. She looked forward to the day when she didn't feel as if she were walking around with a knife lodged in her chest. Thadie gripped the edge of the counter as the machine dispensed coffee into her cup, extending her arms and dropping her head to look at the floor.

Dawn was breaking, and she had to find the strength to smile and laugh with the boys, to be normal. And she had to stop sneaking off to cry. One of these days they were going to catch her and ask her a bunch of questions she didn't want to answer.

What could she say to them? 'I'm crying because your dad doesn't love me. I wish he did.'

Yeah…

No.

'I want this view, for the rest of my life.'

At his deep voice, Thadie screamed, knocking her cup out of the machine and onto the floor. She stared at the broken pieces, the brown liquid on her tiles, scared to lift her head to see if she'd really heard Angus's voice. She might just be losing her mind. And if she was, she wasn't ready to face that reality.

'Don't move.'

Thadie kept her eyes on the mess, and it was only when his arm encircled her waist, when the heat of his big body burned through the material of her short dressing gown—the same one she'd worn when she'd given her infamous press conference—that reality slapped her sideways. Angus was here.

He walked her across the kitchen, lowered her to the ground and pulled a kitchen chair out from under the table. 'Sit,' he told her.

She did, but only because her knees were feeling distinctively wobbly. Thadie watched, bemused, as he dropped to his haunches to pick up the big shards of the broken coffee mug, then mopped up the liquid. Her mouth opened and closed. She didn't know what to say.

So she went for the most obvious question. 'What are you doing here?' she asked. 'Why are you in my kitchen at—' she glanced at the oversized clock on the wall to her right '—five forty-five in the morning? How did you get into my kitchen?'

'I picked up a key from Micah ten minutes ago.'

Micah gave him a key?

Angus reached for another cup, put it under the spout and started the machine. She thought he said something about needing a slug of whiskey but wasn't sure if she'd heard him correctly. Her brain felt as if it had been slapped by a tornado. Whirly and swirly and as if she didn't know what side was up.

'You told me you could only make it back here

to see the boys at month end,' she said, her voice wobbly. 'That's in two weeks.'

'I couldn't wait that long,' Angus told her, grabbing the cup, and dumping a teaspoon of sugar into it. He took a sip, grimaced and placed it on the table next to her elbow.

Right, he had to be missing the boys. That made sense. But could he not have waited until she was dressed, her teeth brushed and with a little make-up on? Or until she was, well, awake?

'The boys will be happy to see you,' Thadie said, dully. 'They've missed you.'

Angus turned around, gripped the counter behind him and met her eyes. His eyes were red-rimmed, his sexy stubble was longer than he normally allowed, and his white cotton shirt looked creased. He looked as if he'd walked in from a hard day at the office: drained and exhausted.

'While I'm always happy to see them, they aren't the primary reason I'm here,' Angus stated.

'Is there a problem with one of your South African clients?' she asked. She couldn't think of another reason he'd fly back ahead of schedule.

Angus folded his arms, cocked his head and amusement lifted one corner of his mouth. 'You could say that. She's been a problem since I first met her.'

Thadie swallowed, realised that her mouth was bone dry and patted the table, looking for her mug. She took a sip of coffee, her eyes not leaving Angus's. He wasn't talking about work, of that she was sure.

'She not only gave me two amazing sons, but she causes my heart to stutter every time I see her. I veer between wanting to hold her, talk to her and take her to bed… That's a lie. I want to do all three at once. With her my world is colourful, without her, it's grey and uninteresting.'

Thadie placed her hand on her thumping heart, thinking it might jump out of her chest. 'Angus.'

Could he be…? Might he be…?

Emotion flooded that normally stoic face and he rubbed his jaw with the ball of his hand. 'The reason that I'm here, at the crack of dawn, is because I don't want to spend another day missing you, not feeling connected to you, not being able to talk to you. You're my best friend, Thadie.'

Oh.

Her face fell. That hadn't been what she had been expecting. For a moment there, she'd expected a smidgeon more than friendship.

Angus scrubbed his hands over his face and closed his eyes, frustrated. 'You can tell that I was brought up in a house where emotions were ignored and love was never discussed, right? I'm making a mess of this… What I'm trying to say is that you are the person who knows me best, someone I trust completely and effortlessly.'

She couldn't discount his words, they meant a lot, coming from a man like him. They just weren't what—

'I'm so in love with you, Thadie.'

Thadie stared at him, her bottom lip between her teeth. 'Say that again,' she demanded, her voice scratchy with hope and joy.

He walked across the room and dropped down to balance on the balls of his feet, his arm on his knee.

He reached up to touch her cheek, his thumb sliding over her bottom lip. 'I'm not good with love words. I was never taught them. But nobody will love you more than me, Thadie. I'll love you fiercely every moment I am with you, for as long as I live. Look, I know I'm not perfect, so very far from it, and that I don't know how to do this—love, relationships, marriage— but I promise I'll learn. You, our boys, will be at the heart of every decision I make, every action I take.'

He rested his forehead on her bouncing knee. 'Be mine, Thads. Please.'

Thadie bent down to drop a kiss on his hair. 'Angus, I've always been yours,' she murmured. He was here and she was home.

He lifted his head and she smiled at him, knowing it might be a bit wobbly. 'I love you too. I'm so very glad you saw my disastrous press conference and thought I needed sorting out.'

He stood up and pulled her into his arms, burying his nose in her neck, and anchoring her to him. 'Ah, I had this plan to flush you from my system.'

She leaned back and laughed. 'How's that working out for you, soldier?'

'Ach, very well indeed,' he replied, before lowering his head to kiss her. His mouth told her a story of passion but also the story of promise, of giving and taking. In his kiss, she was handed pictures of sexy nights and normal days, of watching their boys grow, of whispered confessions and old-age memories. Of spending a life, with all its ups and downs, perfect in its imperfection, together.

Thadie reluctantly broke away and placed both hands on his face and cocked her head to one side. 'The boys are going to come down in about ten minutes and, while there's nothing more I'd prefer to do than kiss you, I need to ask a couple of questions first.'

He nodded, lowered her hands to hold them between them and looked down at her, happiness and joy intensifying his eye colour to turquoise.

Before she got to the scary stuff, she wanted to

assuage her curiosity first. 'The last time I saw you, you said you gave up something you loved for us. What did you mean by that?'

He didn't hesitate to answer her. 'I run and own Docherty Security, as you know. We provide security systems, personal protection officers, do corporate security.'

Thadie knew all this. It was on his website.

'What isn't advertised is that we do kidnap and ransom negotiations. We get those clients word of mouth. But only very few trusted people know I have—*had*—a super-specialised team that takes on sensitive, off-the-books, sometimes dangerous, intelligence-gathering missions for our government and its allies,' he explained. 'Up until a few weeks ago, I went on those missions. Those were the holidays your brothers thought I took. But Docherty Security no longer does covert missions.'

Thadie heard the note of yearning in his voice. 'You miss it,' she stated.

'I do. It was my connection to the military, the way I still served. But doing those missions meant being out of communication for up to six weeks, and they were dangerous. It's something a man who wants to spend his life loving a woman and raising his boys should do. The risks were too great.'

The fact that Angus had given up something

he loved for her, for them, cemented her decision to speak her heart. 'Thank you. Thank you for doing that for us.'

He glanced at the clock and grimaced. 'Anything else? Because we're running out of time, and I want to kiss you again.'

'I want you to get me out of this dressing gown,' Thadie boldly told him, getting sidetracked by the heat in his eyes. He pulled her to him, but she slapped her hands on his hard chest, pushing back. 'But I do have a little more to say…'

He must've heard something in her voice because his entire body stilled, his entire focus on her.

Thadie lifted her hands to hold his face, tears brimming in his eyes. 'While I have no intention of giving up my career, I want us to be a family, living together, raising our kids together,' she told him, parroting the words he used weeks ago. 'I want you to live here, or for us to buy or build another house together. Be my kids' full-time dad, be my partner and my lover and my friend.'

He looked at her, love making him look years younger. 'I could do that, but I have a couple of extra conditions.'

She tried to hold back her huge smile. 'And what might those be?'

'That you marry me in the garden of your childhood home and have the wedding you always wanted. That we limit the number of guests to fifty and go back to Petit Frère for our honeymoon. Deal?'

'Deal,' Thadie replied, not hesitating. She needed to taste that happy smile, so she stood on her tiptoes and placed her mouth on his, winding her arms around his neck, as his kiss turned hot and ferocious. She felt his hand on her butt, showing her how much he wanted her. She couldn't wait for the au pair to arrive: their love needed to be celebrated and she couldn't think of a better way than to do it in her huge bed upstairs.

Their bed.

Angus held her head, and Thadie felt loved and protected, the centre of his world, the perfect, and only, place for her to be.

'Angus! Gus, Gus… Angus is here.'

Thadie let out a groan of frustration. Why couldn't her boys sleep late? Just once?

'Angus!' Gus yelled, running into the room. 'Yay!'

Despite being unable to wrench her eyes off Angus's wonderful face—the face she'd grow old with—Thadie did realise something was amiss when neither of the twins spoke. She pulled back to glance down at them, raising her eyebrows at their folded arms and deep frowns. She sighed. 'What's the problem, guys?'

'Angus is kissing you,' Gus stated, his tone disgusted. 'Again.'

Angus's thumb skated across her cheekbone, and Thadie's knees melted at the love in his eyes. Then he dropped to his haunches, looked Gus in the eye, then Finn, and calmly spoke. 'I'm kissing your mum because I love her and that's not something that's ever going to stop.'

Gus looked a little sick at the thought. 'Ugh.'

Angus's smile was full of mischief, and they exchanged a look. In a decade, Gus would have different feelings about kissing. Angus hugged Gus, but Finn held back. Angus wrapped his arm around Gus but kept his eyes on his younger son.

'Does that mean he's going to be our dad?' Finn asked, his tone serious.

Angus looked up at her, raised his eyebrow and Thadie placed her hand on his shoulder. 'He always has been, Finn. Angus is your real dad, guys.'

Finn looked at her, then Angus, back up to her again. Finally, he nodded and stepped into Angus's free arm. Angus cuddled their sons for a minute, lifted them, and Thadie placed her hands on their little backs, smiling at Angus, tears in her eyes.

She was so crazy happy, insanely in love with her man.

Her boys. Her man.

Her family.

EPILOGUE

THADIE WALKED DOWN the big stairs at Hadleigh House, holding the skirt of her wedding gown off the floor. She and Clara had designed the dress together and it had been made up by Clara's seamstresses. The dress was ivory, in an A-line silhouette, the bodice covered in tiny beads, causing her bodice to glitter. She loved the skirt with its deep ruffles, and she couldn't wait for Angus to see her in it.

Or, honestly, to peel it off her at the end of the night.

'Now, that's a look I should never have to see on my sister's face,' Jago grumbled from the bottom of the stairs. Thadie smiled at him, taking in his simple black suit, and his silver tie.

'You look gorgeous, Thadie,' Micah said, crossing the harlequin floor and carrying a glass of champagne. He turned to look at the twins, who wore long trousers, and silver vests over open-neck, long-sleeved shirts. 'Tuck your shirt back into your pants, Gus.'

Gus looked at Finn before sending his uncle a disparaging look. 'Why are we being punished because they want to get married? Why can't Mum and Dad just dress up and leave us alone?'

'It's a mystery,' Micah wryly replied.

'And why do we have to stay inside?' Finn demanded. 'We want to be with our dad, in the tent outside.'

Micah looked as if he was about to argue but Thadie shook her head, shrugging as she took the champagne. 'If you guys want to go and stand with Dad instead of walking up the aisle in front of me, that's fine.'

The twins grinned and ran across the hall, nearly running into Jabu as he walked into the hall, looking dapper in his black tuxedo. In the garden Angus—and his best man, Heath—stood under the fairy-tale gazebo, waiting for her to walk through the garden to him, her hand tucked into Jabu's arm.

They'd invited fifty of their closest friends, and she'd left the rest of the wedding for Ellie to organise, knowing her wedding was in safe hands. All she wanted was to marry Angus at Hadleigh House, have lots of flowers, great champagne and lively music.

All that was important were the 'I do's. Everything else was the icing on her very delicious cake.

Jabu took the champagne glass Jago held out and they all clinked glasses together in a toast.

'Here's to you, Thadie,' Jago said, his voice deeper with emotion. 'If it wasn't for you and your wedding adventures, we wouldn't have found Ellie and Dodi.'

Thadie pulled a face, thinking how close she came to making the biggest mistake of her life by marrying a man she didn't love. 'I swear, I've actually thought about hunting Alta and Clyde down and hugging them until they couldn't breathe,' she said with a huge grin. 'If they hadn't sabotaged that wedding, I wouldn't be about to marry the love of my life.'

'I hope you're talking about me.'

Thadie whirled around to see her fiancé leaning against the frame of the enormous front door, looking spectacular in a black tuxedo jacket, and wearing his clan kilt. She placed her hand on her heart, for a moment not able to believe that she was going to marry this gorgeous man.

She handed him a wide smile. 'I'm not sure, he's supposed to be waiting for me at the altar in the garden,' she teased him.

Love radiated from his eyes. 'And he will be, I promise. But he seems to have acquired two brand-new, three-foot-high groomsmen.'

Angus walked across the hall to her, clasped her face in his hands and shook his head. 'You look breathtaking. I can't wait to marry you.'

He gently kissed her lips, before stepping back and snagging the champagne glass out of her hand and lifting it in a toast. 'Here's to you, the almost Mrs Docherty.'

'Le Roux-Docherty,' Thadie pertly reminded him as he drained her glass of champagne. 'Hey! I was going to drink that.'

Angus tossed her a grin and briefly placed his big hand on her stomach.

'You can't drink alcohol, remember?' He stepped back, his hands loosely holding his silver sporran, laughing as Jabu spluttered and her brothers laughed.

'See you at the altar in—' Angus tapped his watch '—exactly five minutes.'

It took her ten. Mostly because she had to waste valuable time reassuring her overprotective brothers and Jabu that she was only baking one new Le-Roux-Docherty cupcake. They couldn't, they earnestly told her, cope with another set of male twins.

Thadie laughed, knowing that they absolutely could, that they'd love the challenge. But no, as they'd found out yesterday, she was having a girl, much to Angus's delight. He had this crazy idea that she was cooking a sweet, docile, angelic pink child but Thadie instinctively knew their princess was going to be more of a handful than her ever-mischievous older brothers combined.

Her family had no idea what they were in for.

Genuinely, she couldn't wait for the rest of her life…

* * * * *

Loved The Twin Secret She Must Reveal?

Don't miss the first two instalments in the Scandals of the Le Roux Wedding miniseries, The Billionaire's One-Night Baby *and* The Powerful Boss She Craves.

And check out these other stories by Joss Wood!

How to Undo the Proud Billionaire
How to Win the Wild Billionaire
How to Tempt the Off-Limits Billionaire
The Rules of Their Red-Hot Reunion

Available now!